DEAD AS A DODO

WONDERLAND DETECTIVE AGENCY BOOK 1

JEANNIE WYCHERLEY

Dead as a Dodo:
Wonderland Detective Agency Book 1
by

JEANNIE WYCHERLEY

Sign up for Jeannie's newsletter:
www.subscribepage.com/JeannieWycherleyWonky
Dead as a Dodo was edited by Christine L Baker
Cover design by Ravenborn Covers
Formatting by Tammy
Proofing by Johnny Bon Bon

"Detective Constable Liddell, isn't it?" A soft male voice, originating somewhere just behind my shoulder, somehow managed to infiltrate my thoughts.

Slumped over the bar with my chin in my left hand, I flicked my eyes to the right. A weasel-faced man with long, lank, mousy hair and a stubbly beard was regarding me with something akin to curiosity. When I blinked and tried to focus on him, he pulled his thin lips apart in the semblance of a smile. The two front teeth from the top of his mouth were missing, exposing an excess of red gum.

Ugh. I shuddered and returned my attention to my glass, twirling the remains of the colourless liquid around the ice cubes. I was knocking these shots back a little too quickly. The ice hadn't even had time to melt.

"I don't think I've ever seen you in here before."

The man was annoyingly persistent.

I tutted and swung about on the stool to snap at him. "Inspector!"

"Pardon?" The little man cringed away from my sudden ire.

"It's Detective Inspector." My voice rang out in the otherwise quiet pub. A number of the other patrons, otherwise minding their own business, turned to stare at me.

Fiddlesticks.

"Was," I added, my words slightly slurred. "It *was* Detective Inspector. I've retired now."

"Oh." That seemed to satisfy him and the onlookers. They turned their attention back to whatever dastardly deeds and dark deals they were quietly plotting, but unfortunately my new friend was made of sterner stuff. He would not be put off.

"You seem rather young to be retired."

Was this guy for real?

I tried to ignore him and instead held my glass up to catch the attention of the young bartender. He busily wiped glasses with a filthy cloth and studiously avoided eye contact.

"I hope they gave you a pension."

I swivelled to look at Weasel-man again, not sure whether to laugh or smash a bottle over his head. *A pension?* I'd walked away. They weren't going to offer me a pension. "That's a good one," I said, but I didn't smile.

Thirty-two going on ninety-two. That's how old I was feeling. Losing my partner Ezra, DS Izax, in the way I had, while on a job down in East Devon, had finished me off. I'd been with the Ministry of Witches Police Department for thirteen years, and on their magickal murder squad for eight of those. I'd become jaded even before that final investigation, but I hadn't been remotely ready for the emotional toll that the death of a partner can take.

Part of me didn't understand why I had struggled so badly. When you're on the job, you have to be prepared to make sacrifices, give your all. There is an ever-present danger. Perhaps I'd been lucky. Until that day at Whittle Inn, I'd never been personally affected by anything at work. I'd always compartmentalised everything. Personal life in one box, work in another. But after Ezra's death, I realised that my personal life box was empty.

Ezra had been *it*. The sole content of that stupidly small box.

Not that we were lovers or anything of that kind. There'd been quite an age gap between us, given that he was nearly thirty years older than me. We were just friends. *Good* friends. Buddies. He'd started as my mentor, but I was young and ambitious and determined to have an interstellar trajectory to the top echelons of the Ministry of Witches Police Department. Soon enough I eclipsed him in rank, and I'd been due another promotion that would have pulled me into a different squad. He had been thinking about retirement. We'd been preparing to say our goodbyes.

I hadn't figured they'd be eternal ones.

My eyes filled with tears. I sniffed hard and slammed my glass down on the old wooden bar top, sending a couple of chunks of ice spinning over to the bartender's side. Weasel-man cowered away from me —*by cripes he was jumpy*—but the bartender, obviously long-suffering for such a young man, looked up and raised an eyebrow.

"I'll have another." I jiggled the glass in his direction, pleased I had his attention at last.

His gaze lingered on me a little longer. I knew what he was thinking. I'd had enough. I should go home and sleep it off.

I did my best to glare at him, but I suppose hostile drunks are something he was used to in his line of work, because he shrugged and reached for the bottle of Blue Goblin vodka I'd been favouring. He expertly poured a single finger's worth into a new glass, added fresh ice and a slice of lemon, and slid it over to me. I thought about asking him to fill the glass completely, or even leave me the bottle, but I knew how much money I had in my purse and how little I had in my bank account.

I was going to need another job. And soon.

I twiddled with the vodka, sloshing some of the precious liquid over the bar. Countless numbers of drinks had been spilled here over the centuries. I could imagine the ghosts of patrons past squinting over my shoulder and studying the optics. Little sparkles of light demanding attention out of the corner of my eye.

I refused to acknowledge them. I had no time for the dead.

"It's unusual to see your kind in Tumble Town," Weasel-man said.

I turned my head to glare at him again. *Was he hitting on me? If not, what did he want?* "Are you still here?" I growled.

He climbed up on a stool next to me, as though I'd invited him.

I rolled my eyes.

"This is my local," he said. "I've never seen you here before. That's all."

There was a simple reason for that. I'd been trying out a different pub every night since I'd handed my warrant card over to my boss. There wasn't an inn or a tavern that I hadn't visited in all of London. Probably. Tumble Town had been a bit of a last resort given that it existed on the dark side of town. This particular pub, The Pig and Pepper, had been way down on my list of places to patronise. I'd been living in a comfortable apartment close to Celestial Street, where the Ministry of Witches was located. My local was The Full Moon. But there's a limit to how much you want people you know—people you've worked with, respectable people —to see how much of a drinking problem you have.

Located on the east side of Tumble Town, itself renowned for housing those rogues and villains of the paranormal world—you name it: witches, wizards, warlocks, faeries, goblins, mages, sages, soothsayers and anyone else who didn't want to be found—The Pig and Pepper was a den of iniquity. A cauldron of chaos.

Good people, or people who had nothing to hide, did not tend to hang out in Tumble Town unless they had been born here and had no choice.

I'd had occasion to work on a couple of investigations here, but I'd never been assigned to the Dark Squad, as my colleagues and I thought of them. The Dark Squad were detectives who moved among the rogues here, who understood the people and could distinguish between the worst excesses of witchcraft and magick and general criminality. My understanding was that there was a fine line and that the residents of Tumble Town could get away with so much more than they might out in the ordinary world.

Most of my work had been out in the mundane world, investigating murders that involved magick up and down the United Kingdom.

Weasel-man was looking at me expectantly. I'd zoned out for a second.

"You've never seen me here, but you know my name." That much had filtered through my alcohol-addled brain.

"I knew Detective Izax. I saw you with him from time to time."

"I see." I took a sip of my drink, wincing at the burn in my throat. Good stuff, this Blue Goblin. Clean. But boy, it packed a punch. "Then you know he's dead."

"I heard." Weasel-man nodded.

Of course he had. Nothing ever escapes the attention of the Tumble Town telegraph. It's hard to keep a secret in a town where people trade in such things. Secrets and lies. The most prosperous of the residents are the ones who know the most about those who don't want anyone to know anything about them.

I waited for Weasel-man to tell me Ezra had been a good man. A decent man. A man who hadn't deserved what had happened to him, but Weasel-man said nothing. Maybe he didn't believe Ezra *had* been a good man. That was refreshing in itself. We're all flawed, after all. Or maybe he simply liked to keep his thoughts close to his chest.

If that was the case, Weasel-man was wise.

The clanging of a bell behind the counter startled me. About the size of my head, I was sitting too close to it. My head spun.

The bartender dropped his hand. "Last orders!" he shouted, and I sensed rather than heard the shuffling of punters reaching for their wallets or digging into their pockets to find some change.

"Is that the time?" Weasel-man asked. A hypothetical question if ever there was one. Of course it was the time. How many bartenders get the time for last orders wrong? "I have to be somewhere."

I wondered where he had to be at eleven at night, but I couldn't be bothered to ask. My interest in other people and what they chose to get up to was at an all-time low.

"See you again," he said, slipping off his stool, but I barely even acknowledged him. He tapped the bar twice with his knuckles, a long-honoured Tumble Town tradition that recognised the bartender's service and was a form of goodbye.

Should I have a refill? Funds were tight. I had to walk home and, while it wasn't a long way from here to my pad—perhaps a twenty-minute walk—meandering through the maze of Tumble Town's tiny lanes and alleys could be difficult enough when completely sober.

I sighed.

As if reading my mind, the young man behind the bar plonked down a mug of coffee in front of me. "On the house," he said and offered me a small jug of milk.

I stared across at him, trying to read his face, but it remained closed. Not the slightest hint of warmth.

"Cheers." I quickly drained my vodka and picked up the ceramic mug. There was a chip in the rim. I scratched at it absently with my thumbnail, waiting for the steaming liquid to cool down enough so I could drink it. People came and went, making orders at the bar, bringing back glasses, tapping their goodbyes. I zoned out again, the noise and the light becoming blurred, tears falling unbidden into the dark liquid in the mug between my hands.

"You have to help me."

I lifted my head, struggling to focus, becoming aware that I'd been crying. Just how out of it was I? The pub was virtually deserted now—just a few people finishing off a game of pool at the rear of the pub and a table of poker players loitering over the dregs of their drinks.

"Detective Liddell?"

I slowly swivelled my head. Weasel-man again.

"I thought you'd gone." The coffee in the mug had cooled to the point that a thin layer of skin had formed on the surface. I took a swig. It was strong.

"I need your help," he repeated quietly, and this time he took hold of my right arm and tugged as though to hurry me along.

I glared down at his hand. "I wouldn't do that if I were you, pal." He wouldn't want me to practise my witchy-police-detective-ninja skills on him, I was sure of that.

He dropped his hand. "Please come!" His voice, quiet but insistent, finally got through to me. I'd heard that tone before. Too many times. Laced with dread, but also … need. *You have to sort this out for me. I can't cope with this by myself. Something terrible has happened.*

"What's up?" I asked and took a deep gulp of my coffee. It was habit. Fortify myself with caffeine. No matter how disgusting it was.

"It's my friend." Weasel-man pointed at the door to the street outside. It stood ajar. I could see shapes moving past. "Wizard Dodo. I think he's dead."

CHAPTER 2

I n my experience, going out into the fresh air after a night on the beer can go one of two ways. Either you start to sober up and think a little more rationally, albeit with a buzzy head, or you pass out on the pavement. Luckily for me, that night at least, I did the former.

I followed Weasel-man out into Tudor Lane, one of the oldest parts of Tumble Town as far as I was aware. The buildings faced each other across the lane here, no more than eight feet apart. Even during the day there was little in the way of light. At this time of night, most of the illumination came either from the windows of the houses—mostly three-tiered Elizabethan builds, all wattle and daub and black and white fronts—or the gas-powered lamps that hung from iron struts above our heads.

So, there was lighting ... but it was muted. All the better to hide those who loitered in the shadows, watching me.

I could sense them there, the curious and the antagonistic. It occurred to me that maybe Weasel-man was setting me up. Perhaps this was a trap. Maybe there was a potential cop killer tucked away in the safety of the darkness ...

But probably not. I'd always been one to trust my instincts. Weasel-man was agitated and afraid. He hadn't been this emotional while trying to draw me into a conversation in The Pig and Pepper, which suggested that something had happened in the ten minutes or so after he'd left me.

I wobbled after him—hey! I never said I had sobered right up!—as he turned left out of the pub. He moved quickly and kept to one side, hugging the wall as he walked, as though he too wanted to avoid being seen. The vodka had made me brave, or foolhardy—take your pick—so I stuck to the middle of the lane, all the better to spot anyone if they chose to launch a sudden attack on me as I followed him.

We didn't go far. The houses gave way to a row of old shops, the lane widening slightly, which was lucky because the buildings seemed to bow out here. I had a feeling that they would one day meet in the middle above our heads, creating a kind of pedestrian-friendly tunnel like a fifteenth-century shopping mall.

"Detective Liddell!" A voice hissed at me from a doorway. Weasel-man had taken shelter. "Here!"

I tipped my head backwards, craning to get a better look at the ramshackle building in front of me. Some sort of rundown hat shop. I squinted to read the sign, my eyes in and out of focus. The Hat and Dashery. There were no lights on in the shop itself, or on the floor above, but a glow emanated from the small sash windows on the top floor.

"In here," Weasel-man hissed again, even more urgently than before.

"I'm coming, I'm coming," I told him, and reached inside my leather biker's jacket for my mobile. I thumbed the screen, reassured when it lit up. Better to be safe than sorry. I slipped it into my side pocket where I could reach it easily and drew out my police issue wand. The one I should have returned, weeks ago.

I joined Weasel-man at the door and nodded, indicating he should go first. I might have been drunk, but I wasn't stupid. There was no way I wanted him behind me. He crept up the first flight of stairs, surprisingly feather-light on his feet. In contrast, my tread was heavy and I struggled, catching hold of the banister several times to stop myself from falling. The tread on the carpet was worn, making it slippery, the stairs themselves so old they angled downwards. You risked breaking your neck if you weren't careful. I had cause to thank my sensible footwear—a pair of army boots I'd bought from the army surplus shop years ago—and the fact that I wasn't the type of woman who wore heels.

You can't chase after a villain in stilettos, no matter what you see in the movies.

At the top of the first flight, I paused to listen. Weasel-man had gone on ahead. There was a single door to my left, the faintest of chinks of light threading beneath it, but no sound and no hint of movement. Satisfied that there was no-one waiting to spring out at me, I continued to the next landing. The stairs wound back on themselves, becoming ridiculously narrow at the top. Fortunately, the lights were on in the room beyond and I could see where I was going.

I stumbled into the room, ducking at the last moment to save banging my head on the low doorway, blinking into the light. The floorboards were oddly spongy beneath my feet, and that, on top of the vodka and the steep climb, made me feel a little queasy. I stood still for a moment, took a few deep breaths and glanced around at my surroundings.

Having worked for the Ministry of Witches Police Department, believe me, I knew all about clutter. I had walked away from a desk where the in tray was two feet high. The out tray had hardly existed. Instead, that was where I kept my 'in progress' files. I'd had boxes and boxes of evidence piled high next to my desk and against the wall behind me. Such had been the general chaotic nature of my desk, I'd barely had room for my computer mouse, let alone the computer itself.

But ... and I hesitate to say this ... it had been orderly chaos. I could have put my hand on anything because I knew exactly where, amongst all the disorder, I could find what I needed.

Perhaps Wizard Dodo had been the same. But who could tell?

There were three sash windows on one wall, about two feet wide and four feet high, with a number of dead plants and piles of books decorating the sills. On the back wall, a door led into a room beyond. On every other inch of available wall space there were bookshelves and cupboards. Hundreds and hundreds, if not thousands, of books and pamphlets covered every available surface. Masses of magazines were piled high wherever there was somewhere for them to lean. Several wastepaper baskets were full to overflowing, and drawers and boxes scattered on the floor with their contents spilling out.

The elephant in the room, of course—although it would have been impolite to call him so in life—was Wizard Dodo himself. He was seated at a large oak desk. A desk so big it had to have been built in situ; I could see no other way for it to have been brought into the room. The desk, just like my work desk of old, had evidently been stacked high with files and folders and piles of paper, but quite a few of these piles appeared lopsided and perhaps they had spilled their contents onto the floor around the wizard. There were several mugs and a bottle of brown liquid on the desk along with a couple of dozen coloured pens scattered about.

Wizard Dodo was sprawled back in his chair, his head tipped over his chest, his arms hanging loosely by his sides. I couldn't see any obvious injury.

Gathering my wits, I carefully navigated my way through the piles of paper on the floor and slipped two fingers beneath his chin, feeling for a pulse.

There wasn't one.

"He's dead alright," I confirmed.

Weasel-man emitted a heartfelt wail.

I surveyed the desk once more and leaned over to sniff at the contents of the mug on the coaster nearest the body. The words 'Mean, Moody and Magickal' were emblazoned on the side in purple sparkles. *Mean, moody, magickal and murdered*, I thought to myself. I couldn't smell anything off about the contents. Some sort of herby tea, I decided.

Cold.

Crouching down, all the better to see the wizard

from a lower level, I tried to get a better look at his face. He had an impressively bushy beard. Mid chest, there were a couple of drops of blood, beading there. I picked up a pen from the desk and gently moved his whiskers aside. A circle of blood bloomed on his chest, but not much bigger than a fifty pence piece. He hadn't been shot. This was a stab wound, the entry point unusually small.

I stood up again, ignoring the steady drumming of pain in my temples, and cast around for anything that might have been the murder weapon. A slim knife of some sort? A knitting needle? What about a sharpened pencil?

I couldn't spot anything obvious. "Hmmm."

Weasel-man, waiting at the door, nervously rubbed his hands together.

"Did you touch anything?" I asked him.

He shook his head. I noticed how pale his face was.

"Nothing at all?" I wanted to make sure.

"Nothing."

"Right." My head began to thump harder. I suddenly wished I hadn't consumed the entire supply of Blue Goblin at The Pig and Pepper. I could really do with another coffee. "Did you call the police?" I asked.

Weasel-man started as though someone had

attached electrodes to his backside. "Call them? Why would I call them? You *are* the police!"

Hadn't he been listening to me? "I told you, I'm not," I reminded him. "Not anymore."

He wafted a hand at me as though that were a small and meaningless detail that didn't bear consideration.

I slipped my hand into my pocket to retrieve my mobile. "I need to call them."

Weasel-man took a step backwards in alarm. "Do you absolutely have to?"

"You cannot be serious, mate." I indicated the wizard. "I can't leave him here much longer. The neighbours will start to complain about the smell."

"They probably wouldn't notice," Weasel-man replied, his mouth pulled down at the sides.

I knew what he meant. The east side of Tumble Town could be particularly fragrant at times, almost as though the drains struggled to cope with all manner of hideousness being flushed down there. And given the types of businesses in the neighbourhood, there was every chance there was some particularly unpleasant stuff ending up in the sewers below us.

And then there were the inhabitants. Weasel-man himself looked like he hadn't washed in a while. I could clearly see a ring of grime around his neck.

I examined my phone screen. I had a single bar.

"The reception here is shocking," I grumbled, then lifted the phone to my ear and placed the call directly to the murder squad's central desk. "I need to report a murder," I told them. They knew me. They would set the wheels in motion straight away. "It's above a hat shop in Tudor Lane," I confirmed. "Hat and Dashery or something."

When I was done, I replaced my phone in my pocket. "They'll be here soon," I told Weasel-man. He shivered and his eyes darted to the stairwell.

I could sense he was going to do a runner. Quickly I asked, "Back in the pub earlier, when they called last orders, you told me you had somewhere to be," I remembered. "Was this where you were coming?"

Weasel-man nodded, his eyes flicking around the room.

"What were you—"

I didn't get any further. The sound of a door slamming downstairs tipped my companion over the edge. Without a word, he took to the stairs. I chased after him, but his coattails were disappearing around the bend as I reached the top. I pulled up, knowing without a shadow of a doubt that if I tried to go after him, in my slightly-more-than-slightly-inebriated state, I would trip on the stairs and break my neck.

"Hello?" A woman's voice. I waited where I was and, after a moment, a head peered around the edge of the banister below and squinted up at me, her hair a frizzy halo of silvery curls. "Hello?"

"Hi," I said, and for the first time in months I wished I had my warrant card on me. I could have flashed it at her and made her disappear. Not magickly. Just back to where she had come from. "DI Liddell," I told her. "You are?"

"Hattie Dashery."

Seriously?

She climbed a couple of steps towards me. "I'm the landlady."

Was that really her name? "I see. Would you mind waiting—"

She continued coming towards me. "I run the shop on the ground floor and live in the flat on the first floor."

"So you let this floor to Wizard Dodo?" I asked, gesturing behind me.

"Yes. He uses it as an office. He lives elsewhere. Is he alright?" She was six steps below me now, craning her neck to look beyond me. A woman in her late fifties or early sixties, I surmised, not particularly tall but with an impressively large and matronly bosom and ample hips.

I decided it would be best to keep the scene as clear as possible, so I began to descend towards her, blocking her access and her view. "I'll have to ask you to go back inside your own apartment, Ms ... er ... Dashery. If you don't mind?"

"I only saw him earlier. Are you sure he's alright?" She studied me for a moment and then her face blanched. "Oh my. He's not hurt, is he?"

I hated this aspect of what had been my job. "I'm really sorry," I told her, and gently waved her down the stairs.

"By the goddess ... he can't be dead?" She began to weep.

"Let's go downstairs and put the kettle on," I suggested, taking her gently by the elbow and steering her away from the top floor. This would kill two birds with one stone. I could grab another coffee and ensure she didn't contaminate the murder scene. "While we wait for my colleagues"—I crossed my fingers at the little white lie, the insinuation I was still a detective —"you can tell me all about Wizard Dodo."

"You shouldn't be here, Liddell," Detective Chief Inspector Monkton Wyld snapped at me. We were standing on the cobbles outside The Hat and Dashery. I watched glumly as the pathologist entered the building.

"I just happened to be in the vicinity," I said.

Monkton cut his eyes to The Pig and Pepper a few doors down. "A good night, was it?"

I flushed and saw the spark of regret in his eyes.

"I can smell it on you," he said, more quietly. We were surrounded by my old colleagues, most of whom had been friendly enough when they spotted me. Only one or two had averted their eyes, refusing to acknowledge me, but Monkton Wyld couldn't do that, even if he wanted to. We went way back. Way, way back.

"Did you find the body?" he asked.

"No." I needed my bed. I shouldn't have allowed myself to become involved in this. "I was having a quiet drink, and some random chap started chatting to me—"

Monkton raised his eyebrows.

"Not like that," I snapped. *What did he take me for? How long had he known me?* "He knew who I was. He was just saying hello." *The way an irritating wasp says hello in late autumn.* "He left. A few minutes later he came back and asked me to help him."

"How many minutes later?"

I pushed my hair out of my face, stalling for time. That was a question I couldn't honestly answer. Not with any confidence. I settled on a figure. "Ten minutes."

"So you followed him up to the flat and found the wizard dead?"

"Yes. And then I called you." I smiled, telepathically trying to remind him that I had been helping him out.

"And this man in the bar? Did he have a name?"

Had he told me his name? I couldn't recall. I hadn't been interested in learning it. I shook my head. "I didn't get his name."

"Must have been an interesting conversation," Monkton said.

I glared at him. "He was short, maybe five foot three. Mid-twenties but rough looking. Long, lank hair, brown. Grey eyes. Missing both his top front teeth. Thin, pinched face. Skinny build."

Monkton snorted with derision. "That description could fit half the inhabitants of Tumble Town."

"You know that's not true," I said.

He ignored my protestation. He'd never really enjoyed taking on jobs in Tumble Town. I remembered that from old. That's why he sounded so snarky. "What happened to this friend of yours?"

I shrugged. "He didn't want to stick around when I phoned you lot." I could imagine that Weasel-man had plenty to hide.

Everyone in Tumble Town had something to hide.

"He heard a noise on the stairs and was off like a rocket." Before he could ask about the noise, I quickly added, "That turned out to be the woman downstairs."

JEANNIE WYCHERLEY

"Ah, yes." He consulted his notes. "Hattie Dashery?"

"That's her."

He sighed. "She's priceless."

For the first time, I smiled. I had to agree. "A little bit eccentric, maybe." Her flat, when I'd led her back downstairs to await the police, had been a revelation. The woman was obsessed with Alice in Wonderland— the books *and* the characters. Everywhere I'd turned, there was another cushion emblazoned with the Cheshire Cat's smile, or a teacup and saucer with one of John Tenniel's illustrations. There were posters on the wall of scenes from films and the well-known cartoon. Even the wallpaper! It had a heart and jam tart motif. I'd imagined that might have been specially designed for her. "Harmless, though."

"You don't fancy her for it?"

"Monkton." I levelled my old boss with a tired stare and explained patiently, "As you can see, I'm a little the worse for wear. I wouldn't trust my own judgement if I was ordering from the kebab menu right now. I have no idea whether she's worth looking into." I remembered her tears. "She was shaken up, though. Genuinely."

"Noted." Monkton flipped his notebook closed. "I'll circulate the description of the other fellow you mentioned." I could tell from his voice he didn't hold out much hope of finding Weasel-man, not in the network of lanes and back-alleys hereabouts. "I'll have someone come and take a statement from you tomorrow, if that's alright."

"Okay," I said. I didn't want to have to go into my old office, so someone visiting me would be a better option.

"Are you still at the same address?" he asked.

"For now," I said, and turned my nose for home.

CHAPTER 3

I was still sleeping the Blue Goblin off when the doorbell rang the following morning.

I say 'morning', but it was nearly midday. The insistent ringing of the bell—like someone was leaning against it with their shoulder—told me that I'd slept through the first couple of polite rings.

I sat up and rubbed my head. I didn't feel too bad, all things considered. I'd drunk a litre of water after I'd arrived home before collapsing in bed. Now I urgently needed to pee.

The doorbell buzzed again. It went on for what felt like hours.

Gritting my teeth, I grabbed my robe and raced for the door. "Hang about!" I called. Out of habit, I peered through the spyhole. Monkton Wyld cocked his head on the other side. He'd decided to take my statement himself.

I drew back the locks and threw the door wide. "Come in!" I said. "Make yourself at home. I'll be right back."

"I'll put some coffee on, shall I?" he called after me.

"Do that!" I told him as I disappeared.

I joined him in the kitchen a few minutes later. I'd had a quick wash and brushed my teeth, but he put me to shame. He looked fresh, clean-shaven and smelled of sandalwood or something similar. I eyed his smart suit with his neatly pressed shirt while I tied a knot in the belt of my grotty old bathrobe.

I waited for him to say something about the state of my home. The pile of dishes heaped up in the sink. The laundry dumped next to the washing machine. The clutter on the worktops. Old pizza boxes, Chinese takeaway trays, fast food bags. The shrivelled houseplants. The muck encrusted around the bin.

For the first time in a long time, I saw myself and the way I was living through someone else's eyes. It wasn't pleasant. The problem was, since I'd lost Ezra, no-one else had been here in my home. No-one had visited me at all. The realisation of how lonely I was, of how lost, took me by surprise. My eyes filled with tears and I brushed them quickly away.

"I hate to see you like this," Monkton said, his voice gentle.

I opened my mouth to make an excuse but stopped. Excuses are for losers. Until Ezra's death, I'd never been one to wallow in my misery. I'd been a police officer and a darn good one. I'd always stepped up and taken responsibility.

"It *is* pathetic," I acknowledged. I moved to the sink and began to organise the dishes into a pile next to the draining board, looking for a pair of mugs. As I filled the washing-up bowl with hot soapy water, I looked at him properly for the first time. I could see the concern in his eyes, the soft smile of understanding that curled his lips.

"You're allowed to hurt," he told me. "Ezra was ..." He searched for the right words.

"He was a wonderful detective, funny, intuitive and organised. He taught me so much. I was a better police officer because of him." I scrubbed at the mugs, ferocious in my attempt to remove the rings from the china. "But more than all of that, he was my best friend."

"Why don't you access some help?" Monkton asked, and his tone was delicate.

I shrugged. "You know what it's like," I told him. "We police officers are supposed to be hard as nails. We can't admit a weakness."

"*You* can't, you mean."

"What good would it do? I just need time to get over it. As you said, I'm allowed to hurt." I presented him with the clean mugs and turned to my fridge. Much as I'd feared, there was nothing edible in there. The mould on the cheese looked like it might try to attack me if I came anywhere near it with a knife. I slammed the door closed. "Is black coffee okay?"

"Works for me." He poured the liquid into the mugs and I gratefully reached for one. *Oooh, the smell of fresh coffee when you really need one to kickstart your day*.

"All I'm saying is that with a little professional help, you could come back to us. Get back on the job."

I winced, not wanting to have this conversation.

"I know I could swing that for you," Monkton continued, oblivious to my discomfort. "We could call your absence a 'sabbatical' and, once you're feeling like your old self—"

"And I've given up the booze, you mean?"

"Well, there's that ... but you could talk to a counsellor and I could discuss the situation with human resources, and then you could come back to work. Gradually."

"Gradually?"

"Yes, you know. They have these schemes where

when you've been away sick for a while, you come back on reduced hours and progressively build up."

"Uh-huh." I pretended to give it some consideration. It sounded great in theory, but I had a feeling that once I was back in the office with a dozen fresh cases on my desk, I'd soon be back to full speed.

I just didn't think I could do that anymore.

Yes, I could go back. It would be calm for a week or two. Then they would allocate me a new partner. It would be some rookie who I'd have to worry about all the time. If something happened to them ...

I shivered.

"Let me think about it, Monkton." I raised my coffee mug to him. "Thanks though. You've been really supportive."

"I'm happy to help."

I sat up straighter, took a deep breath and forced a smile. "So! Are you taking my statement?"

"That's what I'm here for." He cleared a place on the worktop to stash his coffee mug before reaching into his pocket for his phone, his notebook and a pen.

I dutifully answered all of his questions and repeated my description of Weasel-man.

Once he'd finished asking questions, and the pot of coffee had been emptied, he flipped his notebook closed. "Thanks for that."

"I'll keep my eyes peeled for my companion if I visit Tumble Town again," I told him.

"No need," Monkton smiled. "We have him in custody."

"You do?" That surprised me. "Why didn't you say so?"

Any criminal worth his salt, let alone a murderer, could have disappeared into the bowels of Tumble Town, never to be seen again. If you were *really* desperate, there were anonymous warlocks who could create a portal and instantly transport you out to the far reaches of some dim, distant continent.

For a price, of course.

"He walked into the station first thing this morning."

I remembered how jumpy Weasel-man had been. "Has he admitted it?"

"It's just a matter of time, I reckon."

"Did he have the murder weapon on him?"

Monkton rolled his eyes. "What do you think?"

I laughed in disbelief. "I'm guessing not." I folded my arms and leaned back against my kitchen counter. "Are you looking into other leads?"

Monkton narrowed his eyes at me. "There are no other leads to look into."

I hunched my shoulders up. *What? Then find*

some, my dear Monkton, I wanted to say. But it wasn't my place to tell my old boss how to do his job.

He waggled a finger at me. "You've got that glint in your eye, Elise. Just remember, you're on sabbatical. Leave this to us."

"Hmpf." *I'm not on sabbatical, I'm finished. Forever done with the Ministry of Witches Police Department.* "You're right," I told him. "It's up to you what you do and what you believe, but me? I don't think it was him."

"According to your statement, the timing was perfect."

"Maybe." I thought back to my first glimpse of Dodo's office, fighting to make sense of my befuddled memories. Yes, Weasel-man wouldn't have needed much time to get there, do the deed and run back, but I'd been on the scene quite quickly afterwards, and it struck me that Dodo had been dead a little while longer. His neck had been cool to the touch, and while factors such as the ambient temperature of his environment would have affected that, it also suggested he'd been dead for longer than five minutes.

But I was no forensic pathologist.

"He was a police informant." Monkton broke into my thoughts.

"Who? The wizard?"

"No, your friend. Maybe that's why you know him."

But I didn't know him. He knew me. There was a difference.

"What's his name?" I asked.

"Bartholomew Rich."

I'd never heard of him.

After seeing Monkton out, I collected the post from my box in the lobby and traipsed back upstairs. I surveyed the mess strewn about the place. My whole flat looked like a bunch of pixies had taken up residence and invited their stinking troll friends around for a week-long party.

This is not me. Monkton's right. I need to get a grip.

I brewed more coffee and drowned myself in a long bath while I drank it. I couldn't imagine that swapping Blue Goblin for a caffeine habit was a particularly sensible idea in the long run, but caffeine and I were good friends. We had a history that went a long way back. Show me a detective who can work such impossibly long hours without some sort of crutch.

I'd become a coffee connoisseur of sorts. Brazilian, Columbian, Indian, Sri Lankan, Costa Rican—I'd tried and loved them all. My favourite, oddly enough, was some Vietnamese mix that a friend had brought me back after a holiday there one time. By crikey, that stuff could coat your innards, but I liked it strong.

Once I'd hopped out of the bath and drained the coffee pot, and decided against brewing a third batch, I chucked a load of laundry in the machine and began to clear up. Switching to autopilot, I let my thoughts meander around my mind in unison with the chug and tumble of the washing machine. By the time I'd made it through two loads of clothing and cleaned the kitchen and living room from top to toe, filling three black bin bags with rubbish, one thing was abundantly clear to me.

Bartholomew Rich, Weasel-man, was not Dodo's killer.

I don't know why I thought that way. I had no definitive proof, but I considered myself an excellent judge of character. Bartholomew Rich was afraid of his own shadow for some reason, but he wasn't a murderer. All I'd seen in his eyes was curiosity and gentleness. I'd given him short shrift when he'd spoken to me at The Pig and Pepper, but all he had wanted was a little company, I suspected.

I could understand Monkton's angle. Rich had walked into the MOWPD this morning—unusual in itself as it was on the 'right' side of the tracks in Celestial Street rather than in Tumble Town—and voluntarily offered himself up as a person of interest.

My suspicion was that Rich was hiding from someone. And where safer than a police cell?

As darkness began to fall, while I waited for a frozen meal to heat up in the oven, I sat cross-legged on the sofa and began to work through the pile of post that had been building up over the past six weeks or so. Circulars, sympathy cards, a couple of notelets from my Mum.

Bills.

I had direct debits set up to cover everything. The problem was, now that I was out of a job, I had no income. I'd defaulted on several payments without even realising it.

Including the rent.

I slumped against the back of my sofa and looked around the room. I'd been living here for six years. A two-bedroomed apartment on the fourth floor of a decently maintained building, with a small lounge and kitchen. It had a tiny Juliet balcony where I'd imagined I would like to sit on summer nights and moon gaze. I could remember being thrilled to find this place; the neighbours were quiet and respectable, and it was just a stone's throw from Celestial Street and my office. Indeed, the proximity to the Ministry of Witches is what made this place a des res.

But I'd never really moved in properly. There were boxes stacked in the spare bedroom and the corner of the living room waiting to be unpacked. In all this time, I hadn't obliged. Why had that been? Too busy? My job had kept me busy, travelling the length and breadth of the UK to investigate murders.

Or too lazy? On my days off, as rare as they had been, I had either slept or shopped or met up with friends.

Or had I known that although I referred to this place as home, it would never really *feel* like it?

In the end it had just been a place to lay my head after a long day on a case, or after a few days away elsewhere in the country, hunting down criminals or interviewing suspects or witnesses. Most of the time I hadn't even cooked here. I'd grabbed a takeaway, fallen asleep in my clothes and then showered the following morning, making myself ready to head back out again.

The truth was, this apartment had become an expensive bedroom. I could no longer afford it. I either needed a new job or I would have to downsize. And quickly.

Perhaps Monkton was right. Maybe I should consider going back to the murder squad.

I curled my lip in dismay. Anything but that!

Perhaps it was time to look around and see what else I could find.

CHAPTER 4

I clutched the latest copy of *The Celestine Times* to my chest as I ambled along the cobbles on Tudor Lane. My feet were killing me. I'd been parading around Celestial Street and its neighbourhoods all morning, dropping off my hastily constructed CV to places advertising for staff. I'd tried offices, only for each of the managers to gaze in disgust at my jeans and motorcycle jacket and rainbow-streaked hair. I'd fared no better at bars and restaurants, although here the problem had been that I didn't have any experience. Finally, I tried a butcher's. The plump old gentleman there in his red and white stripy apron had worried that I was a little young.

"I'm thirty-two," I'd protested.

"Exactly," he'd said, folding his doughy arms and thereby ending our dialogue before it had even started.

"That's discriminatory," I'd grunted, and he'd shown me the door. I went quietly. You can't argue with a meat cleaver, can you?

The other purpose for my ramble around the paranormal enclave safely tucked away from the curious eyes of the mundane in central London had been to try and identify new apartments to rent. Most of the ones on the 'right' side of the dark–light divide were way too expensive for me. At my grand old age—no matter what the butcher thought—and having been independent for so long, I didn't fancy a flat share. That meant seeking out cheaper areas.

Namely Tumble Town.

I couldn't quite see myself living there, to be honest, but nonetheless, I'd had a look at one place from the outside, discounted it on account of its grim facade, and somehow just continued to walk east. Eventually, as though I had contrived to do so, I found myself on Tudor Lane.

I paused outside The Pig and Pepper. The bartender was the same young man who had been serving two nights previously. On an impulse, I walked in and strolled directly to the bar. He was busy with a pen but, when I peered over the counter, I realised he was working on a giant crossword puzzle. He looked up and clocked me.

"Do you remember me?" I asked.

"Nope." His reply was automatic.

I pointed at the bar stool furthest away from the door. "I was sitting there, the evening before yesterday."

"No, ma'am," he repeated.

"I'm looking for the man who came in to talk to me. Yay high." I demonstrated with my hand, a whole head shorter than me. "Lanky brown hair, sharp nose," I elucidated. I wasn't seriously looking for Bartholomew Rich because I knew exactly where he was. Languishing at Her Majesty's Pleasure. I simply wanted to do a little digging.

"Ma'am, if I don't remember you, then I'm definitely not going to remember who you were with," the young man said, perfectly politely. He dropped his pen and picked up a cleaning cloth instead. He carefully wiped the counter in front of me even though it was pristine. When he was standing directly in front of me, he leaned a little closer. In a soft voice he told me, "If you don't want trouble, you won't ask your questions around here. No-one knows anything. No-one gives anyone up."

I nodded to show I understood.

"Would you like a drink?" he asked me, his voice louder now. "I've replenished my stocks of Blue Goblin."

He *did* remember me.

I stared at the bottle of vodka hanging upside down on its optic. Terrible was the temptation. But what good would it do me? I'd just sink further into the morass of misery I'd been creating for myself.

"I'd kill for a coffee," I said.

He indicated his coffee pot. "I can oblige."

I was tempted but I had other plans. "Another time." I turned to leave, but something occurred to me. I stopped and glanced back at him. "Did I even pay you for the coffee the other night?"

He smiled. "You can owe me," he said, and winked.

I nodded. He seemed like a decent guy. I could work with him. "I don't suppose there are any jobs going?"

"Here?" He sounded surprised by my question. "I'm afraid not. Unless you want mine?"

"You're leaving?"

"As soon as I can find something else."

"What sort of work are you looking for?" I asked, imagining he would say actor or musician or something exotic. But no.

"Anything at all as long as it doesn't involve tipsy witches or bellicose wizards," he said.

Musing on the bartender's wordsmithery, I meandered a little further along Tudor Lane. I tried to tell myself I was just out looking for jobs and apartments, but who was I kidding? There were still a few hours of daylight left—what little filtered through the gap between the leaning roofs above—and the atmosphere was generally calm. There were plenty of people around, coming and going; women with baskets of shopping, gentlemen with packages or their hands in their pockets, kids racing around and chasing each other.

And the others.

'The others' were the problematic residents of Tumble Town, the ones who hid themselves away in the murkiest corners. It would be too easy to say they were all thieves and tinkers or cut-throats and pirates, but there was an element of truth to that.

As if that wasn't unnerving enough, there was also a realm of people who lived … well, who knew where, to be honest. These were the shadow people. They menaced Tumble Town's residents after dark. They were everywhere, and it was claimed they saw and heard everything.

But what they looked like, who they were, from where they originated and what they wanted? I had absolutely no idea.

"Hello again, dearie."

I snapped back to reality. A woman stood on the

step of The Hat and Dashery, the door open behind her, the shop bright and welcoming.

I blinked, recognising her thanks mainly to her impressive bush of silvery curls. "Hattie! Wow." She didn't resemble the woman in her pyjamas I'd met on the stairs the other night in any way, shape or form. She was dressed in a beautifully tailored yellow jacket, complete with fob watch, a starched cream shirt with a flowery cravat. She was also sporting the most wonderful top hat I had ever seen, in a luminescent lime green, decorated with felted fruits—bananas, oranges, apples, grapes and plums—and finished off with an enormous red gauze bow. Her head took up almost the entire width of the doorway.

"Wow?" she queried, as though her appearance was a surprise to no-one except me.

"Your hat! It's just incredible!"

"Thank you," she smiled. "I make them myself, you know." She indicated the shop behind her, the shelves and tables laden with all manner of colourful creations. I had the urge to go in and browse. "Do you think it might have been more fitting for me to wear black?" she asked, her voice trembling. "I considered it, and I do have some stunning funeral hat creations, but ... I don't think Wizard Dodo would have approved somehow."

I smiled in sympathy. I could see, beneath her immaculately made-up face, the strain that had taken its toll. There was a tightness around the eyes that gave it away. I was familiar with that look in my own mirror. I swept back my hair a tad self-consciously. I was badly in need of a trip to a hairwitch for a cut and recolouring. The rainbow effect of my streaks was fading.

"You look beautiful," I said, seeking to reassure her.

"Have you come here to visit your colleagues?"

"My colleagues?"

"Yes." She pointed upwards. Most of them have finished. Thank goodness. Up and down the stairs they were, all day and all night." She faltered. "Late last night ... they took his ... him away."

I reached out and squeezed her shoulder. "I understand it's intrusive to have all those people stamping up and down your stairs, but they are doing the best job they can."

She shrugged. "The Ministry of Witches don't really care what happens to anybody in Tumble Town though, do they? We're not high up on the agenda when it comes to justice."

I didn't know how to respond to that. I have to say that in all my years on the force, it had never occurred to me that we discriminated against half of London's paranormal population, but now I was beginning to see things in a different light. I could have uttered some banality about how that wasn't the case, but I decided that would merely add insult to injury. I dropped my hand and forced another smile. The side door, the one that led up to the apartments above the shop, stood ajar.

I nodded at Hattie. "I'll see myself up," I said, and slipped through the door as though I had every right to.

This time, sober, I navigated the uneven stairs more easily. The lights were blazing above the landings, and my ex-colleagues had set up some temporary lighting too, no doubt having struggled to get up and down the narrow stairs themselves. Hattie's door was firmly closed so I carried on to the top floor, climbing the steepest flight of stairs. As soon as my head cleared the banister, I peered around the edge, crossing my fingers that someone amenable to my presence would be in situ.

I was in luck. DC Cerys Pritchard was on her knees, sorting through some paperwork. I'd known Cerys a long time, since she'd transferred from Aberystwyth. We'd worked some interesting cases together and sunk a few bevvies in bars afterwards.

"Hey," I called quietly. I couldn't see whether she had company or not.

She looked up with a start, her short black hair framing her pretty face, then smiled at me. "Hey yourself!" She tidied up the papers and stood, brushing dust from her black trousers. She was a small woman, and slim. But she was tough enough. "I heard you called this in."

"I did." I climbed up the last few stairs, ducked under the low doorway and joined her in Wizard Dodo's office. The windows had been opened and a large amount of the floor cleared. Cardboard boxes had been brought up to store evidence as it was gathered. It looked like it had been a big job. "Is all this being taken back to the station?"

"Quite a lot of it." Cerys puffed out her cheeks. "Although I'm not sure what the point is, to be frank."

"No?"

"They have someone in custody. I hear he's likely to confess."

I frowned. "Bartholomew Rich."

"That's the guy." She noticed my face and grinned. "Uh-oh! I know that look, Elise."

I grinned. "Am I that transparent?"

"You don't buy it then?"

"I don't, although hand on my heart, I can't tell you why."

"The famous Liddell instinct," Cerys teased me.

How I wished I hadn't been quite so blotto on the night in question. What had I missed? If my faculties had been sharper ...

"Are there no other suspects at all?" I queried, glancing around the office as though I would spot a clue that my colleagues had missed. My fingers itched to start turning things over, reading the pieces of paper on the desk, rummaging through the contents of drawers.

But it wasn't my place to do that anymore.

"None." Cerys held up a finger, wrinkled her nose and sneezed politely. A delicate little 'chee' sound. "Sorry, it's all the dust." She dabbed at her nose with the back of her wrist. "There are areas of this room that don't look like they've been disturbed for a thousand years."

I laughed. "There's a ridiculous amount of paper-work here. Was it a break-in, do you think? Was the murderer looking for something?"

"By all accounts, our victim was always this messy," Cerys snorted. "I haven't seen evidence of anything missing. Nothing looks particularly ransacked."

But it had to be hard to tell. "What did this wizard actually do here?" I asked.

Cerys pulled a face. "Your guess is as good as mine. You know what it's like when you're working a job in Tumble Town; you can never find anything out. No-one will talk. I think DCI Wyld would be wisest palming this one off on the Dark Squad, to be honest."

I had no doubt that would happen, sooner rather than later. If this turned out to be a case that was going nowhere, Monkton would offload it. The Dark Squad wouldn't be too interested in it either. The death of one wizard would not cause any ripples in the general fabric of our world.

Far better for Monkton that Bartholomew Rich confess. At least he'd have a solved case to add to his stats. That always looked good in the annual report.

"Meh," I said. "Maybe I've got it all wrong. Maybe it *was* Rich. It's not my concern anyway, is it? I need to leave it to you guys."

"We miss you, you know."

"Wyld wants me to come back."

"I should think he does. You're a great loss to the team."

"Thanks, Cerys. That's a sweet thing to say." I reached out and enveloped her in a hug. It felt good to have human contact. To have a friend.

"I mean it," she said, her voice muffled against the side of my head. "We lost a fine pair of detectives the day Ezra was killed." She pulled away and studied my face. "You know, it's just an idea, but if you came back, maybe you and I could team up."

I smiled. "That's worth thinking about." It wasn't. Imagine losing another partner, especially Cerys. That would be as bad as losing Ezra.

No, I wouldn't countenance it.

"I'd better go," I said. "I shouldn't be here at all."

"Let's meet up for a beer or a coffee sometime," Cerys suggested.

"Coffee sounds good. I'm laying off the booze for a while."

"Smart thinking." She winked at me and crouched down again, picking up a sheaf of papers.

I moved to the head of the stairs and paused. "Just one thing?"

"Mmm?" Her head was already back in whatever she was doing.

"Out of interest," I said, trying to remain as casual as I could, "do you have any idea what the murder weapon was?"

Cerys didn't look up. "According to Mickey O'Mahoney's report at the briefing this morning, it was a single stab wound to the heart."

Michael O'Mahoney was the red-haired pathologist with whom our department tended to work most closely. Mickey had a fascination with murder and regularly wrote academic papers and conducted research for the Ministry of Witches Medical Council of Great Britain. His enthusiasm for death was second to none.

As I'd thought. "Like a knife?"

Cerys blew a stray hair away from her face. "Mickey said it would have to be a stiletto blade or a screwdriver or something really thin."

I nodded. That made sense. There hadn't been a lot of blood left at the scene.

"Interesting," I said. She looked up and smiled. I wiggled my thumb and little finger near my ear. "I'll call you and we'll set up lunch or something."

"I'll look forward to it."

"Good luck with the case," I said, and carefully picked my way down the stairs.

CHAPTER 5

E arlier, I'd passed a bakery just a few doors down from The Pig and Pepper. The proprietors obviously baked everything on the premises rather than bought it in, because the smell wafting out of the door and into the alley had made my mouth water. Now I retraced my steps and climbed down three worn stairs into what can only be described as a foodie's paradise.

The shop itself was small, perhaps fifteen feet square, and cut almost in half by the counter that stretched across the middle. The ceiling was low, as though the building was squashing itself, and the floorboards bounced as you walked across them, but given that the structure had been standing here for the best part of five or six hundred years, I didn't think there was much risk of me disappearing into the cellar. The walls were lined with shelves containing cakes, buns, bread, biscuits, pastries, quiches, pies and pasties and all manner of baked goods.

I put on half a stone just looking at it all.

"What can I do you for, darling?" A cheerful woman with bleached yellow hair smiled at me.

"Oooh! Erm ..." She'd caught me on the hop. There was so much choice I couldn't make a decision.

"We have some Chelsea buns fresh out of the oven. Can I entice you with these?" With one gloved hand, she lifted a silver tray, the buns warm and sticky with white icing, the scent of baked currants and cinnamon tickling my nostrils.

My stomach rumbled. I hadn't eaten since the revolting freezer meal the previous evening. "Yes please," I said. "I'll take two, and"—I pointed at her coffee machine—"two coffees, please."

"Coming right up," she breezed, and within a few minutes I was a couple of pounds lighter—of pocket at least—and heading back towards The Hat and Dashery, balancing my purchases on a recycled cardboard tray.

Peering through the window, I could see Hattie slumped in a large wing-backed chair, grandly upholstered in royal blue with gold piping. She looked despondent and small, somehow diminished by her sadness. I tapped on the glass with the knuckles on my left hand to let her know I was coming in, and moved towards the door. She straightened up immediately, plastered a smile on her face and rushed to open the door for me.

"Hi again," I said, stepping through into her immaculate premises. The floor was blonde sanded wood, the walls painted in blocks of deep, bright colours, and all of the shelving and units were made from glass, allowing the detail on the impressive range of hats to be the focus of attention. I held up my tray. "I brought you coffee, to thank you for looking after me the other night."

"I rather think it was you who looked after me," she corrected me, but reached out to take the tray and carefully carried it to her counter.

I followed her. "Your hats are exquisite! This place is something else."

"Thank you. It's my pride and joy. I've been here nearly thirty years, Detective—" I could see her struggling to remember my name. Perhaps I hadn't even told her.

"Elise Liddell," I offered. "But I have to be honest with you," I grimaced, "I'm not a detective."

Her brow wrinkled in confusion and she cut her eyes at me. "But—"

"Not anymore. I used to be. Until recently." I picked up one of the coffees and handed it to her. "I'm sorry if I gave the impression that I was."

"You act like one," she said and flipped the lid off her cup.

"I suppose it's ingrained in me. I worked for the MOWPD for thirteen years. It's all I've ever known."

"Why did you leave?" she asked. "You're young to retire."

I shook the Chelsea buns out of their bag and picked up my coffee, taking a moment to think. I decided to be truthful. "My partner was killed." I took a breath. "And while I was fortunate enough not to witness it, I ... well ... I haven't been coping very well." I left it at that.

"I'm very sorry for your loss," she said. "It isn't easy, is it?"

We stood there at her counter, quietly united in grief. I allowed her the space to think. Sometimes as a detective, allowing others to fill the silence can be most beneficial. Even if they don't talk, their thoughts can betray them.

In this case, I wanted to find a point of communion with Hattie. It seemed to have worked. She indicated a seat pushed against the wall. "Pull that up," she instructed me, and took the one behind the counter.

I did as she said, made myself comfortable and plucked up one of the buns, peeling back a layer of the fresh dough to expose the currants and cranberries.

She watched as I popped a chunk in my mouth. "Did you say your name was Liddell?"

"Yes," I replied, with my mouth full. "You can call me Elise, though."

"Such a wonderful name!" Hattie enthused. "You may have noticed that I am a fan of all things Lewis Carroll?"

"I most certainly had," I said. It hadn't been hard to recognise the obsession when I'd visited her apartment above the shop, and of course the hats were a bit of a giveaway too. A mad hatter, Hattie unquestionably was.

"The character of Alice was based on a little girl named Alice Liddell," she told me, her eyes shining. "The name Elise is very similar to Alice, is it not?"

This had been mentioned to me previously, but I didn't want to ruin Hattie's moment. "Isn't that a coincidence?" I marvelled and pushed the spare Chelsea bun towards her.

"Do you know the books?" she enquired.

"I read them a long time ago," I told her. "My mother teaches English at the Academy of Magickal Arts in Worcester. She's a huge fan of Victorian literature. Me, not so much." I pulled a face. "I could never sit still long enough to read a book as a kid. I liked to be out and about and doing stuff."

She smiled. "I can understand that."

"What about you?" I gestured with my Chelsea bun around the shop. "Have you always been creative?"

She nodded. "Yes. Unlike you, I preferred to stay indoors and work on my crafts. If I wasn't elbow deep in glitter and glue, I wasn't happy."

"Why hats?" I asked.

"My parents were milliners. They had a shop along Knick-Knack Lane for many years. I used to help them out and they apprenticed me, I suppose. It worked out alright for me. I love doing it. When my father passed away, my mother and I bought this old building and moved the business here. She's been gone five or six years now, but I can still imagine her sitting in the big chair"—she indicated the enormous blue wing-backed chair—"and steaming feathers."

Why would anyone want to steam feathers, I wondered.

"It makes them fluffy," Hattie said without looking away from her bun. "They can get a little ragged or dry if they've been stored for a long time. The steam revitalises them."

"Oh." That made sense.

"I used to have the top floor and Mum had the flat directly above the shop. I moved in there after she died and let the top floor out. The income helped with the bills."

This seemed to be the perfect opportunity to steer the conversation back to the murder investigation. "To Wizard Dodo?" I asked.

"Yes. He used it as an office. There's not a huge amount of room up there. The main room, a smaller room at the back where I had a small kitchenette fitted for him, and a bathroom. That's it. He lived elsewhere."

"Do you know where?" I asked, knowing that my ex-colleagues would have already asked these questions but curious all the same.

"16 Bath Terrace. Do you know it?"

I shook my head, mentally storing away the address. "I don't know Tumble Town that well."

"16D I think it is. Was. Well, I suppose he still lives there ... until he doesn't." The thought seemed to confuse her. "Top floor."

"How well did you know him?" I asked.

"How well do any of us know anyone?" She pulled a chunk of Chelsea bun away and dabbed at an errant currant that had fallen onto the paper. "He was an old friend of my father. Dodo used to buy customised hats from him. My father specialised in pointy hats and magickal hoods. You know what wizards are like. They're far vainer than witches. They like their hats to have added sparkle, or stars, or a little something that elevates their costume above the run-of-the-mill.

Wizard Dodo came to my mother's funeral and it transpired that he was a little down on his luck, had moved out of his home and was looking for somewhere to lodge. He hadn't been able to find anything big enough that would encompass his library as well as himself."

She smiled at the memory. "I offered him the flat and, as it turned out, he decided to use that as an office and rent a studio, I think that's what they call it. That's how he ended up in Bath Terrace."

"He did have an impressive library," I said. "What did he actually *do*?"

"Ugh." Hattie wrinkled her nose. "He liked to think of himself as some sort of spellcaster. It's a little complicated ..."

"Go on." I pushed for more information. Most, although not all, witches and wizards were spellcasters, so I didn't find her explanation particularly enlightening.

"He was a spellcasting matchmaker."

I stared at her blankly. "Like a dating agency?"

"No, no!" she giggled. "He didn't match people with other people. He matched people with the spells they needed."

"I don't understand how he would make money doing that." You only had to go Witch Google and you could look up any number of spells. Failing that, the bookshops in Celestial Street sold spell books by the bucketful.

"I know what you're thinking." Hattie waggled a sugary finger at me. "Spells are ten a penny. And they are. But what if you want something a little out of the ordinary? Something your grandmother might have used before modern-day technology? Or something as old as time, maybe? What if you need a spell that the wizards of Ancient Persia might have used, or the witches in Cleopatra's time? Or what if you needed to adapt a spell so it would only work for the person who cast it? Powerful blood magick, perhaps?"

I raised my eyebrows at the thought, and she nodded in evident satisfaction. "That's what he did. He was a clever man, Dodo. Always receiving and writing letters, always ordering things from booksellers around the world and taking delivery of packages. People would come and go all the time. Some of them popped into the shop by mistake because they'd get the address mixed up, and I would point at whichever hat I was wearing and say, 'Do I look like a wizard?'" She snorted.

"So it wasn't unusual for him to receive visitors?" I asked. It wouldn't be easy to pin down potential suspects if he'd been that popular.

"Not at all. All times of the day and night too." She wiped her hands on a tissue and picked up her coffee.

"The only time we ever fell out was when he had late-night visitors. There's no underlay beneath the carpet on the top floor, and those floors are made of hardwood. The sound reverberates above my head when I'm lying in bed."

"How often did you fall out?" It was an innocent enough question for a detective. These are the things you want to find out, but it pulled her up short.

She pouted. "I thought you weren't with the police anymore?"

"I'm not." I sat back on my chair. She had a point. "I'm really not. I'm just …" I shrugged.

"Curious?"

"Exactly that."

She remained quiet for a while, swishing the cooling coffee around the paper cup.

"We fell out a few times," she said eventually, "but not badly. He was always falling out with someone."

"A bit cranky, was he?" I asked.

"He could be. But as long as he paid his rent on time and kept the noise down, I was perfectly happy for the most part. And as I said, we went way back, so I suppose I felt I should be looking out for him."

"So you heard others having angry exchanges with him?" If the floors were as thin as she said, I was hopeful she might finger someone.

"On occasion, yes. Just Sunday afternoon, one of

his wizard friends was in and I heard them having a disagreement. Nothing ferocious. Just bickering. There were plenty of other occasions where I'd hear old Dodo having a moan. But in a neighbourhood like this, there's always someone ready to have a go at you for something."

"Who was the wizard friend from Sunday?" I asked.

Hattie shrugged.

"You can't think of any names?" I pressed.

I spotted a glint of amusement in her eye. "You can't be that naïve, dearie. Everyone's anonymous in Tumble Town."

Of course they were.

"What about the name Bartholomew Rich?" I asked.

Her face remained resolutely neutral. "Never heard of him."

There was a clunk from outside. I turned to see Cerys Pritchard pulling the door to the upstairs closed. She hefted a couple of smaller boxes and set off down the lane in the direction of The Pig and Pepper.

Dodo's office would be empty.

No sooner had the thought crossed my mind than Hattie arched her eyebrows. "You want to go up there, don't you? You want to have a poke around."

I opened my mouth to protest but gave up. Not much point in lying.

"It wouldn't be strictly ethical," I told her.

She reached up beneath the huge gauze bow of her top hat and rummaged for a moment, fighting to free it from her curls. She carefully removed the hat and turned it upside down. Reaching into the sweatband, located on the underbrim, she drew out a key.

"This will open the front door. Once you get upstairs, if you unscrew the newel cap on the top handrail, you'll find Dodo's spare office key. Just remember to put it back afterwards. I'll need that when I rent the office out again."

"I will, and I'll drop this one back to you," I promised.

"If I'm not here just push it through the letterbox," she said. "I have a feeling you may be some time."

She lifted the hat carefully onto the top of her head, angled it slightly and held it there with her left hand while fishing into the pencil pot with her right hand and extracting a long hatpin with an emerald-green jewel decoration.

I watched her stab the pin through both the hat and her hair to hold the oversized creation steady.

My, my. That was a vicious looking weapon.

Wasn't it?

CHAPTER 6

"Genius," I muttered as I removed the newel cap from the post. There was just enough room to stick my fingers in the gap and retrieve the key. I lay the cap on the top of the stairs, where it would serve as a reminder to lock up and leave the key behind when I left.

Unlocking the door, I ducked and stepped into the room. The windows had been closed and the musty smell was back. Boxes were piled high against the shelving units and around the desk. Now the room had been cleared—after a fashion—I could see more of the floor and the thin old carpet that had to be a relic from the seventies, given the garish green and mustard mix.

"Where do I start?" I asked myself as I stepped forward. I moved over to the nearest window. The blinds were open. I couldn't recall whether they had been on the night of the murder or not. I gazed across the gap to the building opposite. A warehouse or factory of some kind, boarded-up at ground level. Because of how the buildings buckled towards each other, the three-storey structure opposite couldn't have been more than six feet away. If I had leaned out of the window—which I had no intention of doing—I might have been able to shake hands with a person doing the same on the other side.

"Eww." I shuddered at the thought of the drop to the cobbles below.

I crossed the room and opened the door. This was as Hattie had described. A smaller room with a single cabinet on the wall, a sink with a draining board and a cupboard underneath, a kitchen table and chair, laden with even more of Dodo's papers and books and his printer. A door in the corner led to a bathroom, in desperate need of updating, as the orange suite testified.

"Nice."

I shuffled through the piles of stuff on the table here. Mostly magazines relating to astrology and a couple of circulars for a psychic fayre, long out of date. Sometimes, in my line of work—my old line of work—it wasn't so much the content of such things that was important, but more anything that had been written on them. There had been several occasions when a hastily scribbled phone number or name had given me the break I needed when working on a murder case.

Knowing that Cerys would have been looking for exactly that kind of evidence while she'd been in here, I wondered if she'd found anything.

Nothing immediately jumped out at me, and I drifted through to the main office. Pivoting slowly, I aimlessly took in my surroundings. "What do I think I can find that no-one else can?" I asked. "And what am I even doing here? This is none of my business."

I eased myself into the wizard's chair. It did feel weird, I have to admit, sitting in the very place he'd died, but I wasn't particularly squeamish about such things. Over the years I'd seen it all and heard it all, and nowadays extraordinarily little caught me by surprise.

From his seat at the desk, Dodo would have had a good view of whoever came through the door from the landing. If the door had been open, he would have seen his would-be killer as they arrived at the top of the stairs.

Had he been taken by surprise? That was difficult to say. What would I have expected to see if he had been taken unawares by his visitor? He might have scattered the items on his desk in shock. The desk had been untidy, but I already knew that clutter was Dodo all over. What he hadn't done was push his chair far away from the desk or stand up. When I'd found him, he still had his feet tucked under the desk.

That suggested to me he hadn't been alarmed by the person who had shown up.

Another factor that went against Bartholomew Rich. Dodo would never have felt threatened by him.

But just because my Weasel-man had been a visitor that night, it didn't mean he'd been the only one.

What if …

I leaned back in the chair. Maybe he'd had several visitors that night. Perhaps there had been several noisy encounters. Hattie had been in her pyjamas when I first met her. Had she been asleep in bed only to be rudely awakened? Had she snapped and marched upstairs with a hat pin and stabbed the wayward wizard?

It was a possibility worth considering. He would have probably remained at his desk, perhaps even chuckling to see this frizzy-haired woman clad in her jim-jams, armed with one of the tools of her trade, standing in front of him and threatening him. He'd known her since she had been a child. How dangerous would she have seemed? Perhaps she'd snapped and lunged across the desk with her hat pin, not intending to kill him.

I shrugged. I wouldn't discount the scenario. No matter how slim, a motive is a motive.

Or what of Bartholomew Rich?

In the time it had taken my coffee to cool, he could have easily come up here from The Pig and Pepper and had a set-to with the wizard. Perhaps he carried a stiletto-type knife as a matter of course. He was a police informant; he must have known some rather shady people. It would make sense to be armed in Tumble Town.

It couldn't have been a prolonged argument, though. And he had disposed of the weapon before he gave himself up.

But that was weird. Why would he do that?

And why come and alert me?

I might not have been firing on all cylinders two nights ago, but he had seemed genuinely shaken up to me.

And why had he trusted me and then done a runner when I called my ex-colleagues?

So many questions, so few answers.

"If only I could interview him," I chuntered to myself, but that was out of the question.

I reached over to the nearest box and opened the lid. This was filled with material from the desk. Post-its and pens, a stapler and a hole punch, notepads, books and magazines, correspondence—dozens and dozens of letters—and Sellotape.

Cerys, or one of her junior colleagues, had neatly

filed all the envelopes together and secured them with a fat elastic band. I pulled them out of the box and tugged the band free, wrapping it around my wrist while I flicked through each letter. I was fairly sure that if there had been anything obvious here, it would already have been removed to the incident room. This was all secondary evidence. It would be photographed and catalogued but probably didn't have much of a role to play in what had happened to Dodo.

But what struck me were the number of stiff off-white-almost-cream envelopes. I pulled one out for a closer look. It had been stamped 'Return to Sender' and the address scored through. I flipped the envelope over to confirm that Wizard Dodo at 125C Tudor Lane had been the original sender.

I plucked the next off-white-almost-cream envelope from the pile. This had also been stamped 'Return to Sender'. A quick perusal of the others confirmed that Dodo sent out his correspondence in these identical envelopes. But more interesting than that, the letters that had been returned to him were all from one person.

Wizard Jamendithas Ironhouse of 3B Clay Court, Tumble Town, London.

Why would Dodo keep sending out letters when he knew they would be returned? Had Wizard Ironhouse moved away?

I placed half a dozen of them on the desk in front of me and twiddled my fingers over them. I shouldn't open the letters. I wasn't a police officer anymore. I'd be tampering with evidence ...

But maybe just one. Who would notice? Would anyone have taken the trouble to catalogue every single letter yet? I didn't think so. It wouldn't matter to them whether this had been opened or not.

I searched around for something to open the envelopes with. A letter opener would have been perfect, but I couldn't even locate a pair of scissors. Eventually I settled on a paper clip. I straightened it out and inserted one end into the ungummed corner and, carefully and neatly, slowly ripped the envelope open.

Inside was a single sheet of matching off-white-almost-cream vellum, neatly folded in thirds. I opened it up and grunted with disappointment. An invoice. That's all it was. An unpaid invoice. The amount outstanding had been £25.00.

"£25? That's nothing," I said. "So why didn't you pay up, Wizard Ironhouse?"

I shuffled through the envelopes, arranging them in date order, and chose a more recent one. Had Dodo been sending out reminders for this bill? There was only one way to find out.

I casually opened a second envelope.

This time the amount outstanding was for £125, for five amounts of £25.00. Each of the individual amounts was dated, and one of those clearly matched up with the other invoice I'd opened.

Wizard Dodo had scrawled a note on the bottom of the page in purple ink. I squinted and turned the desk light on to better enable me to decipher the spidery writing.

Further to our recent conversation, if you would pay your dues I would be most obliged, old chap. You might find a refusal of further credit offensive in the extreme. As you must appreciate, a wizard cannot survive on friendship and good intentions alone.

He'd signed it with the initial E. "Interesting." I pulled out my notebook—I carried one through force of habit rather than necessity these days—and made a note of Wizard Ironhouse's full name and the address that Dodo had been sending the invoices out to, along with the amounts.

It wasn't much, but it was something at least.

I returned the letters to the pile, wrapped the elastic band around them and replaced them inside the cardboard box. Nobody would ever know I'd taken a sneaky look at them.

Then I moved on to the box beneath it. This one seemed to be full of spell books, some that must have dated back to the earliest days of expensive parchment and skilled bookbinders. As I dug deeper into the box, moving some of the smaller volumes around, I realised that Wizard Dodo had owned a fine collection of grimoires. I couldn't know whether he'd unearthed them in one of the numerous antique, curio or junk shops that were hidden down Tumble Town's back lanes, or whether he had inherited them, or come across them in some other manner, but I could imagine that any magickal archivist would have loved to get their hands on Dodo's hoard.

There was a peculiar element of romance and poignancy, knowing that each of these books had been lovingly collated by a man or a woman who had long been dust in a crypt. I grabbed a handful and returned to my seat. I began to flick through the first of these that caught my eye, a green leather-bound volume with lots of loose pages. I waved away the dust that puffed up into the air as soon as I turned the cover and each subsequent page. According to the front page, this was a grimoire belonging to Mary Bethany Pointer, born in 1798.

Outside dusk fell, unnoticed by me. I sat, entranced, reading through Mary's work. She had collected together recipes and snippets of wisdom passed on to her by her mother and grandmother, and, judging by the development of her handwriting and spelling, had kept the grimoire from an early age.

There were fine line drawings of plants and flowers, as well as lists of ingredients for headache cures, muscle strains, colds and flu and women's problems. Later there were a couple of love spells and a fertility spell. I wondered if—and how—that had worked out for her.

Towards the back pages, the writing became smaller as Mary struggled to fit everything into the available space, and there was an increased number of inserts, including, I noted, a pink post-it note with the name Jane Mills randomly scrawled on it in blue biro, in what I took to be Wizard Dodo's writing. The final few pages were blank, and on the inside of the back cover, someone had written Mary's name and the dates 16th January 1798 to 21st October 1882.

"That was a grand age, Mary," I said and gently closed the book. I had a moment, feeling emotionally bereft. The whole of one woman's life on the pages of a roughly bound notebook. "Bless your heart."

Bless yours.

I couldn't figure out whether the words had been spoken aloud or had merely formed in my head. I sat straighter in surprise.

"I must have been having a moment." I yawned and rolled my neck around on my shoulders. It had been a tiring day, but what were my chances of being able to do this again tomorrow? My ex-colleagues might remove these boxes at any moment if they deemed it necessary to sift through the contents more thoroughly.

If this had been my case, I'd have been telling them they *did* need to. I was convinced that somehow, the clues to Dodo's murder would be here.

Somewhere.

With my notebook and pen ready, I opened the next grimoire in the pile, Tobias Frederick Longseed, and began to scan the contents. I had no idea what I was looking for, and there were an awful lot of books in Dodo's office, but it would be an interesting way to spend an evening.

"It's in the drawer."

"Huh?"

I'd been dozing! Now I jumped awake, my heart beating fast, eyes wide.

Somebody had been here, in the office with me, I could feel it.

I'd left the front door unlocked and the door to the office ajar. Perhaps that had been foolhardy, but I'd hoped that if Cerys decided to pay a visit, I'd have advance notice. I cocked my head, listening. I could hear the faint sounds of rain on the roof and the sound of jeering drifting up towards me from somewhere down on the street.

What time was it? Chucking out time at The Pig and Pepper?

I swivelled in my chair, glancing behind me. The door to the back room wobbled on its hinges, a minute movement, as though someone had recently pushed past it. I pulled my wand out of my pocket and quietly pushed myself to my feet, creeping towards the door. It was dark beyond because I hadn't turned the light on. I hadn't needed to; it had been daylight the last time I'd been in here.

Senses straining, I moved gently forward, my body in a semi-relaxed crouch, ready for anything. I flicked the light switch. Nothing happened. The bulb had gone.

"Illuminate," I ordered, and my wand lit up. I shone it into the room and then directed it at the shadowy corners. As far as I could see, everything was as it had been before. That left the bathroom. Out of habit, I glanced behind me once more, then moved on. Clasping the bathroom handle, I twisted and pushed. It swung inwards, revealing ... absolutely nothing.

Just to be sure, I peered behind the shower curtain —still nothing—and tested the window. Locked.

"I'm getting jumpy in my old age," I said and, pocketing my wand, closed the bathroom door behind me and strode back towards the main office. Just as I reached the desk, I heard a whirring noise.

I whirled, yanking my wand out in one smooth, well-practised motion, just like the cowboys of old, targeting the noise. In the back room, a small blue light flashed on a machine. I stole forwards, puzzled.

The printer.

It roared into life and began to spew paper. Sheet after sheet.

I spun about in alarm. Dodo's computer had been taken away, so who was controlling this? Hattie Dashery? From her computer downstairs?

The paper started to overfill the shelf and began to cascade onto the floor. I grabbed for one, crumpling it as I caught it.

It's in the drawer.

Just those few words in a regular font. I reached for another.

It's in the drawer.

And another.

It's in the drawer.

Every single sheet spilling out of the printer had those same four words. *It's in the drawer.*

Finally the printer ground to a halt, the blue light replaced by a red one. Not entirely trusting that it wouldn't start up again, I edged towards the machine to read the flashing display.

Out of paper.

No doubt if I filled the paper tray, I'd be knee-deep in more four-word messages. I looked for an off-switch but there didn't appear to be anything immediately obvious, so I reached past it and turned it off at the socket. For good measure, I yanked the plug out.

"It's in the drawer? What's in the drawer?" I turned round and round. Only a single drawer in this room. I pulled it open, and using the light of my wand, rummaged about. Cutlery.

I returned to the main office and scanned it. Surprisingly there were only two drawers in this room. Both were on the left-hand side of the desk. But I'd already checked them, and I knew they were empty.

I pulled them open again. The top one had an ancient half packet of Beech-Nut chewing gum, a couple of coffee-stained serviettes and a pile of paperclips.

The bottom one had a blob of dried out Blu Tac, a couple of thumb tacks and a lot of dust.

"It's in the drawer? There's nothing in the drawer!" I closed them, one after another, with a sharp slap, suddenly bone-tired. What wouldn't I do for a shot of Blue Goblin right now?

Or something to eat. The Chelsea bun seemed half a lifetime ago.

"It's in the drawer."

This time, in spite of my exhaustion, I was convinced someone had spoken the words.

I shivered. A cold finger traced up the line of my spine to the nape of my neck, where my hair prickled. I had a definite sense of being watched.

Next to me, the blinds at the window rattled.

Just the breeze. Was that what I'd been hearing? The rattling of metal blinds? The windows were old. They probably let in a draught.

But what if someone was trying to communicate with me?

I dropped to my knees in front of the desk and crawled underneath, shining my wand upwards at the underside. In the far right-hand corner, tucked close to the leg, the light from my wand caught a glint. Something metallic. I reached for it, a small lump, and it came away easily enough.

A bronze key, with a series of intricate wards on the bit and a long spiral stem.

I shuffled back out from beneath the desk, almost banging my head when I straightened up too quickly. I remained sitting on the floor and studied the desk. From this angle, it was clear as day. The bottom one of the two drawers should have been deeper inside than it was. I gently pulled it open all the way, and there at the back was a small bronze disk. It pivoted when I touched it with my finger, revealing a keyhole. Now I clambered to my feet in excitement. It stood to reason that the key I'd found would fit perfectly.

It did.

I slid it in the lock and turned it, hearing a satisfying click. By leaving the key in place, I could pull upwards, using the stem and bow as a handle. The bottom of the drawer folded towards me, revealing a secret compartment below containing a single item.

A notebook, approximately six by four inches, with stiff navy-blue cardboard covers, bound by an elastic band. It was battered, the edges of the cover had become fluffy and the pages well-thumbed. This had to be it! The reason why Wizard Dodo had been killed.

But when I opened the notebook, the pages were blank.

"Uh." I tipped my head back on my aching neck. "Give me a break."

In the distance, I heard a clock—possibly the one situated in the dome of the Ministry of Witches building—begin to chime midnight.

I wasn't about to turn into a pumpkin, but I knew I should be thinking about heading home. Tumble Town wasn't where I wanted to be in the wee hours of the night.

But first, I needed to tidy up after myself.

It wouldn't look good if my ex-colleagues learned I'd been second-guessing them.

CHAPTER 7

E ver since Ezra's tragic demise I had struggled with insomnia, but for some reason, that night, I slept like the dead.

It was late morning before I deserted my pit of weird dreams and dragged my sorry self into the shower. Afterwards, I wiped the bathroom mirror clear of steam and gazed at myself. In spite of the fact that I needed a trip to the hairwitch. I thought I looked better than I had in weeks, my face not quite so sallow, my eyes a little brighter.

"You know what it is, don't you?" I mouthed into the mirror. "You've got the bit between your teeth again. You're working on a case. And you love it."

I did.

I couldn't deny the fact that I came alive when I had a mystery to solve. But still I scolded myself. This wasn't *my* case. I wasn't on the job anymore. What I was doing could, at best, be construed as sticking my nose in where it wasn't wanted, and at worst, an obstruction of justice.

In the early hours of this morning, I had been sitting on my sofa with my wand and the small note-book I'd pilfered from Wizard Dodo's office. Of course, I felt bad that I hadn't left it for Cerys to find, but what good would a blank notebook be? It would simply be filed in one of those anonymous cardboard boxes and no-one would take the slightest notice of it.

I'd tried every spell I could think of to get the note-book to reveal its secrets, from the very basic, 'reveal' type spell to some more complicated 'spill-the-beans-sunshine-or-I'm-arresting you' type ones I'd learned at the Ministry of Witches Police Academy. No amount of cajoling or bullying had worked. The magick behind the blankness of the pages stumped me.

Over a coffee, I flipped through the notes I'd made the previous evening. There were a number of names here who would be worth talking to, even if they were just for some background on Wizard Dodo or addi-tional details on what he did for a living. The quandary I was in was whether or not to turn them over to Cerys or DCI Wyld.

I knew I should, although I didn't fancy admitting how I'd come by my information. The more cunning side of me tried to negate the ethics of the situation away by persuading my moral side that what I'd put together might not come to anything. Around ninety per cent of police work is routine and never creates a useful lead. It can be incredibly time-wasting. I might send my ex-colleagues on a wild goose chase and stretch their already limited resources to breaking point.

Wouldn't it be better for me to test the water first, so to speak? Just to get an inkling of where the land lay? If I could find something that would positively pan out into a strong lead, I'd be in a better position when I had to admit I'd been investigating the murder scene without the MOWPD's knowledge or consent.

I felt the rush of blood through my veins at the thought of tracking down the names on my list. I'd been born to be a detective. Bar work and butchery, bookshops and offices? Those kinds of jobs were not for me.

The question was, should I take up Monkton Wyld's offer to return to the department or not? The lead weight in my stomach every time I thought of doing so suggested it wouldn't be a good idea.

But that left me still needing a way to make money ... and to do something that would satisfy my need to poke around in other people's affairs.

"Like an unofficial detective," I said, sitting on my

bed to towel between my toes. "Like a ... oh!" I caught my breath. "What a nitwit!"

I dropped my towel and stood up, slapping myself on the side of my head. "Not an unofficial detective! A private detective! Ooh! Ooh!" I hopped around, wondering what to do first. Towel myself off or google how to get a private detective licence.

If there was such a thing.

"I could do that! I have great contacts, both paranormal and mundane." I danced around, yanking open my drawers looking for clean clothes, most of which were in the ironing pile. I settled on a pair of leggings and an oversize t-shirt. "I'll need an office ... and business cards ... and, wait. An office? Where will I get the money to rent an office?" I looked around my apartment, my eye settling on the dining table where my laptop was set up. "I could work from here."

But that wouldn't work, would it? I would need walk-ins, clients popping by. It had to be somewhere accessible, and unfortunately, my apartment block was like a fortress. My neighbours would be less than pleased to have undesirables traipsing up and down the stairs at all hours of the day and night, because—make no mistake—I knew I'd be putting in the hours.

That's what I did. I devoted my life to my work.

I slumped in my seat. Office space in London went for a premium. That was particularly true in the area around Celestial Street. All manner of magickal accountants, lawyers, architects, surveyors, doctors and dentists had hung their plaques around here. The cheapest option was to rent a desk by the hour, but again, that really wouldn't work if I had clients coming and going.

No. I'd have to have a good think about what was possible and how best to proceed.

What difference does it make, anyway? I asked myself. *It's not like I have any clients. I should worry about office space when I actually have a client I need to meet.*

And that in itself was a bit of a problem. Where would I find clients? I guessed I'd have to advertise. Maybe I could find a trade journal of some kind. No, wait! A newspaper would be good! *The Celestine Times* for starters.

But that would cost money too.

Unless I could get some publicity for free. I knew some of the reporters. I just needed a story to pitch to them.

First things first. I needed a case. If I hadn't solved any cases, who would want to pay me for my services?

I'm going round in circles. I tapped my wand on my coffee cup and watched it refill itself. *Although ... if I solved the Wizard Dodo case before the police, that would be a boost, right?*

Except, the police investigated crimes because that was their job. A private investigator investigates on behalf of a client. I sipped my coffee, good and hot and strong, just as I liked it. It would look better if I was solving a case on behalf of a client.

I needed a client.

I sat up with a jerk, spilling coffee down my clean t-shirt. It didn't matter; I was going to have to dig out a suit anyway.

It appeared that all roads led to Bartholomew Rich, after all.

Witchwood Scrubbs.

I paused outside the world-famous gates to stare up at the oval plaster reliefs. A man and a woman gazed back down at me, their neutral features permanently set in stone.

HM Prison Witchwood Scrubbs, nicknamed 'Witchity Grubbs' by Londoners in the know, is the main prison for paranormal beings in the south of England. Operated by the Ministry of Witches Prison Service on behalf of the British Crown, it houses both male and female prisoners in its six wings.

This wasn't the first time I'd visited, not by a long way, but it was my first visit as a 'civilian'. I'd made a few phone calls and pulled in a few favours. Fortunately, I had a long list of people with previous indiscretions who owed me for keeping their secrets. It hadn't taken much wrangling on my part to be rewarded with an emergency visitor's pass.

Once at the visitors' entrance, I deposited all of my valuables when requested to—including mobile phone and wand—and observed as they were stowed away in a locker. At the inner gate, I had to hand over my notepad and stubby pencil to a guard—he examined it suspiciously, probably considering how much damage I could do with it—and then submit to a thorough pat-down by a female prison officer before standing in front of an x-ray machine. This was all part and parcel of life as far as I was concerned, and I didn't even flinch.

I was shown through into the empty visiting room and took a seat at one of many scuffed tables. I deliberately chose one in the centre of the room. The guards would stand against the walls, and this was the furthest I could get from them. As I waited for Bartholomew to be brought down, I gazed around at the grubby white-washed walls, the barred windows, the worn floor, the tired notices on noticeboards. So much grey everywhere. So little light.

And the smell. I could never get used to it. Baked beans and fried chips. Tired clothes. Cheap shampoo.

The stench of four hundred incarcerated convicts who, somewhere along the line, had chosen a path that put them at loggerheads with ordinary paranormal society.

That took some doing, I can tell you. Paranormal beings forgive a lot!

Bartholomew Rich turned up in a prison-issue grey —of course—tracksuit that was at least two sizes too big for him. He had to keep yanking at his waist to stop the bottoms falling down, and the cuffs on his sweatshirt had been rolled up several times so as not to drown his hands.

Other than that, he was much as I remembered him. Lank hair, although a little cleaner than a few nights ago, thanks to the availability of showers in the prison, and a stubbly chin beneath a thin face. His eyes brightened when he saw that his mysterious visitor was me.

"Detective Constable Liddell!"

I waited for the prison officer to remove his hand-cuffs so he could sit down.

"Have you come to take another statement?" he asked, his eyes flicking to my notebook.

"In a manner of speaking." I glared at the prison officer, hovering behind Bartholomew. "Any chance of a couple of coffees or something?"

"It's not proper visiting hours," he said, as if I

hadn't realised that. If it had been, there would have been a tea and biscuit trolley.

The rotten jobsworth.

"I know that," I told him. "But my throat is as dry as a chip." I changed tack and offered a winning smile. "Please?"

He grunted. "Alright."

"Thank you," I said, my voice laden with as much saccharine as I could muster.

I dropped my gaze back to Bartholomew. "How are they treating you?"

"Yeah, fine. You know how it is." He shrugged.

I didn't really. I'd never spent time in the nick, only observed it from the other side. "You've been inside before?"

He nibbled on the nails of his right hand. They'd been bitten down to the quick and looked sore. "On remand. A few times. Nothing serious."

"You know the ropes, then? That's good."

He eyed me quizzically. "You've come to ask me more questions about the other night, have you, Detective Liddell?"

I nodded. Time to get down to business.

"Remember in The Pig and Pepper I told you I wasn't a detective anymore?" I asked, keeping my voice quiet. I didn't want to be overheard.

"Yeah. Yeah." He sniffed and swiped at his nose

with the back of his rolled-up cuff. I noticed he'd caught the skin of one of his fingers when he'd been biting his nails. He was bleeding.

He mistook my grimace of sympathy as a look of disgust. He sniffed harder. "Rhinitis," he told me.

I decided to ignore that. "The thing is, Bartholomew—may I call you Bartholomew?"

"Well, you can if you want. But no-one else does, like."

"What do they call you?"

"Snitch."

"Snitch?"

"Rich the Snitch. On account of my line of work."

"Right." I considered this. It didn't seem like a particularly nice name to have. "What do you prefer to be called?"

He stared at me blankly. "Snitch."

I widened my eyes slightly. "You *like* to be called Snitch?"

"It's a name."

I couldn't argue with that. I took a breath and started again. "The reason I'm here, *Snitch*, is because I've decided to go into practice as a private investigator."

"Ooh!" This must have met with approval because he perked up. "Like *True Detective*."

The way he said that sounded slightly sordid.

"Mmm. Like a proper professional detective but not affiliated to the police."

"But you will still be on their side?" Snitch narrowed his eyes. There was no fooling this chap.

"On the side of law and order, I suppose, yes. I want to see justice done."

Snitch pouted.

"But—" I hurried on, "I'll take clients. So I get to pick and choose which cases I investigate. And I will investigate a situation at the client's behest."

"The client's behest. Yeah." Snitch nodded knowingly, then frowned and added, "What does that mean?"

This could prove to be a long interview. "If you agreed to be my client," I told him, trying my best to be patient, "I would investigate the circumstances of Wizard Dodo's murder and clear your name."

Snitch's eyes darted to the right, where a prison officer leaned against the bars, staring out of the window. "I didn't do it," he whispered.

"I believe you," I said. "That's why I'm here."

He dropped his hands onto the table between us and spread out his fingers. He desperately needed moisturiser on those cuticles. "I didn't do it," he repeated, softer now. I leaned forward so I could hear him. "But I'm better off in here."

"Why?" I asked.

He rolled his eyes towards the prison officer again and clamped his mouth shut.

"Will you be my client?" I prompted him.

He gave a slight shake of his head. "I don't have no money."

"I understand that. But *I* don't have any clients. What I'm proposing is that I take your case for free."

"Free?" Snitch sniffed hard and ducked his head, looking out at me behind surprisingly long eyelashes. I could tell he thought there would be some catch involved.

"Completely free. You need all the help you can get, and I need to build up a reputation. It's a perfect partnership."

"A perfect partnership." Snitch repeated the words to himself. "I like that." He glanced at the prison officer again, and then round at the empty tables.

I wondered what he was thinking. "So, what do you say?"

"The thing is, Detective Constable—"

"Inspector," I replied automatically, then caught myself. "But you can call me Elise."

His eyes grew big at this. "Elise?"

I nodded.

"That's a pretty name." He looked pleased, like a child who's just been told he can have an ice-cream if he behaves. "Okay." He swiped at his nose again. "Like

I was saying, the thing is"—he leaned toward me and, once again, I came closer until we were within head-butting distance—"I really liked old Dodo. I'd never have done nothing to hurt him, but I'm ..." he trailed off.

"You're frightened," I acknowledged. "I get that."

"What if somebody comes after me?"

Why would he think they would? Unless he knew something or had seen something. "I'll do my best to protect you."

"Right." He didn't sound convinced.

"If you truly liked Dodo, you'd want to see his killers brought to justice, wouldn't you?" I wasn't averse to a little emotional blackmail.

This time he sounded more resolute. "Yes."

"Then you have to tell me all you know," I told him. "The only way we're going to get you exonerated—"

He pulled a face; I could see the confusion there.

"We need to prove you didn't do it," I clarified for him.

There was a long silence. I let him do his thinking in peace. He slumped over the table, rubbing his eyes with the heels of his hands, his right knee jigging nervously. I wanted to reach out and touch his shoulder, just to soothe him a little, but I knew that wouldn't go down well with the prison officer.

At that moment, the other officer arrived with two plastic beakers of coffee. I drew back as he placed them in front of us, along with a pair of wooden stirrers and a handful of packets of sugar.

"Thanks," I said, genuinely grateful. I desperately needed coffee. Although right now, as I sweated over whether I'd reeled Snitch in, a hit of something stronger wouldn't have gone amiss.

Snitch watched the prison officer walk away to join his colleague. When they started to talk to each other in low voices, he sighed and turned back to me.

"Alright. I'll do it."

I hid my jubilation. At last! A proper reason for investigating Dodo's murder without sneaking around behind my ex-colleagues' backs. "You'll tell me everything?" I asked.

Snitch regarded me seriously. "I will."

I pulled my notebook towards me, the coffee forgotten. "Let's get started, then."

CHAPTER 8

"I had an appointment to see Wizard Dodo—"

"An appointment? An official one?" I cast around my cluttered memory, trying to recall a diary or planner or some other means of organising a schedule. I couldn't remember seeing anything. Perhaps the police had already removed that before I had a chance to snoop.

"Kind of," Snitch said. "He told me to come over at eleven."

"That's right." I vaguely recalled Snitch having to dash off. "When you say he told you to meet him, when did he do that? When was that discussed?"

"Earlier that day."

I chewed the top of my pencil and fixed Snitch with a look. "The more specific you can be, the more I'll be able to uncover."

Snitch rolled his eyes. "It felt early to me. I hadn't been up long. I don't do mornings. Not on purpose. The early alarms in this place are killing me." He shot daggers at the officers as though they were personally responsible for the prison regime.

"Focus," I told him and reached for my coffee.

"So"—he ran a quick mental calculation—"it was probably around one. I like to get a pastry from Betty's Bakery if I've got the readies on me. It was busy, the bakery was. It always is at that time of day. I got me a cheese and bacon slice." He licked his lips. "That's the problem with being in here. The food is rank."

"And?" I grimaced at the coffee—Sheesh! That would tar your insides—and reached for the sugar.

"Wizard Dodo was there too. He liked their doughnuts. We walked back to his office together."

I pricked my ears up. If what Snitch was saying was accurate, then this was useful. I could begin to create a timeline. Dodo would be dead ten hours later. I just needed to fill in the blanks in between.

"And how did he seem to you?"

Snitch thought about that for a moment, then tapped the table. "You know, now that you ask, he was a bit irritated."

"And this irritation? Would you say that was out of character for him?"

Snitch giggled. "Strictly speaking, not really."

"What did you talk about?"

"He asked me to pop by later."

I tapped my pencil on my notebook. "I could do with a better idea of who he was. Tell me about him."

Snitch turned the corners of his mouth down as he reflected. Eventually he said, "He could be a bit crotchety, could Wizard Dodo. A bit of an old nark at times. You wouldn't often catch him smiling or laughing. If there was something to complain about, he would be first in line, you know?"

"I dated someone like that once," I said, shuddering at the memory. "Never again. So, you wouldn't say he was a pleasant person? He tended to rub folk up the wrong way, did he?"

"That's just it, he didn't really. We all knew him. We knew what to expect. There was a kind of gentleness to his gruffness, if that makes any sense."

It did. I had known several people like that. "How long had you known him?"

"Since for always!" Snitch looked at me in surprise. "I grew up in the same house where I live now. He was always around, although not in the office above the Hat and Dashery. I began running errands for him around the lanes when I was knee-high."

"I see." That made sense. "And that's what you did for him? Run his errands?"

"Yes, around Tumble Town, mostly. I would fetch

and deliver packages and drop things at the post office for him. Get his shopping in if he was too busy. As he got a bit older, I found myself doing more of those sorts of things for him."

Snitch sniffed and swiped at his nose again. This time I sensed the wave of sadness.

"I won't be doing that for him no more," he said wistfully. "I'll miss the old codger, I will."

I reached out and patted his wrist. "I know how that feels."

"Ahem!" One of the prison officers coughed loudly. I darted a startled glance at him and then, remembering the no-touching rule, shifted back in my seat and fiddled with my notebook.

"I know generally what he did—dealing with spells and such—but can you fill me in a little more about that?" I asked.

"Probably no more than what you've heard. From my perspective, I'd say he trod a fine line between various schools of magick. On the one hand, he dealt with white magick, harmless stuff, love spells and things of that sort—he used to get a lot of requests from all around the UK and abroad for that kind of thing. That was his bread and butter so to speak. You know, a hastily printed out spell and instructions, a list of ingredients, that kind of thing. All for the bargain price of a tenner."

"Uh-huh."

"Then, on the other hand, there are all sorts of goodwill spells and medicinal spells and recipes for potions and things that the wizard would find in all those grimoires he had. He was always on the lookout for those, and with each new one he found, he would go through them quite carefully and copy those spells. He would send me off to the bookshops dotted around Tumble Town and beyond—Charing Cross on occasion—to look for new ones. I think he had some huge index of spells somewhere, but I might be imagining that?" Snitch tapped the side of his forehead. "He knew lots. Kept it all up here. Imagine! All that knowledge just disappeared when he died."

"Those sorts of spells would cost more?" I asked.

"Of course. Anything he had to spend more time digging around for, he would charge more for."

"And what kind were the most expensive? Do you know?"

Snitch wiggled his head. "There was the darker stuff. Some of it *really* black. I don't know what sort of spells these folks were after, but much of it involved a lot more research, and that's when Wizard Dodo would be at his grumpiest. He would say he could do something in a specific timeframe and then he'd have to deliver on his promise. I don't think it was always as straightforward as that. He was working for some pretty twisted folk at times. I know that because I've hand-delivered their parcels. There's places in Tumble Town where *even I* fear to tread, and as I say, I've lived here my whole life."

"Were there ever any requests for spells that he wasn't able to deliver on?" I asked curiously. What if he'd made a promise and not delivered? That would be a motive, wouldn't it?

"Not that I know."

"Was anyone ever threatening towards Wizard Dodo?"

Snitch shook his head. "Not in my hearing."

"Would you be able to give me the names of people he created spells for?" I asked, but had to hold back a smile at the look of horror that crossed Snitch's face.

"Are you crazy? Absolutely not."

I pushed his coffee towards him.

"Tell me about that night."

Do you remember the rain?

It was coming down outside and I'd got my timings wrong. When I'd seen the wizard at lunchtime, he'd asked me to call at eleven. I think the plan was I'd collect some deliveries to drop off locally and walk him home. The Hat and Dashery was in darkness, and so were Hattie's windows, but they were on in the office above. I went in the side door and climbed up the stairs all the way to the top.

That was the standard thing to do. Hattie has a lock on her apartment door so she leaves that side door open while the wizard is at work. He locks it up when he leaves. I know that because I've sometimes walked him back to his flat on Bath Terrace.

I mean, not that he needed assistance from me, really. But I was useful to him to carry his packages and I suppose, if I'm honest, he liked company. Not especially *my* company, like. Just *any* old company would do.

But I do, too. You know? None of us likes to be alone.

But that night there was someone up there already.

As I climbed up the final flight of steps, I could hear this person talking about a particular spell he needed, but it must have been something obsolete because Wizard Dodo sounded ... well ... grumpier than normal. He was trying to explain that locating such a spell would take time and would therefore cost a little bit more.

I wasn't bothered by someone else being there. I've lost count of the number of times I've just hung out in the back room while the wizard attended to business. Sometimes I made tea and coffee for him, and if he ever *had a printer jam, he knew I'd be able to clear it for him. I'm good with things like that for some reason. I don't know why, because I've never used a computer in my life. But technical gadgety things—bizarrely I seem to be a natural when it comes to fixing them.*

Anyway ...

They stopped talking as I arrived on the landing. Wizard Dodo was at his desk, facing me, but I couldn't see the other chap. He was behind the door, maybe standing at the bookcases. The wizard held a finger up to me like a schoolteacher, to stop me in my tracks kind of thing.

I waited for a minute and the other person in the room said something like, 'You promised complete discretion.' Yeah, those were the words, I think.

At that, Wizard Dodo looked back at me. 'You're early,' he said, snappily like.

I was going to apologise, but he didn't give me the chance to speak. He shot his finger at the door, and it slammed in my face.

I was a bit put out by that, I must confess, but I figured he was discussing payment for a job and wanted privacy so I made my way downstairs and back into Tudor Lane.

I ...

I was debating on going home but I didn't know what time it was. I don't have any heating there, whereas The Pig and Pepper has fires burning no matter what the weather and Wootton, the young fella behind the bar—I knew he'd know the time. So I went in there to hang out with the guys playing pool for a while. One of them bought me a drink. We just chatted and what have you.

I was getting ready to head back to see Wizard Dodo when I spotted you at the bar and I remembered you from when you used to hang about with Detective Izax. He was a good man. I liked him a lot. And you seemed really sad, sitting there all alone, so I figured I'd say hello.

And it was nice talking to you.

Then Wootton called last orders and I thought I might as well go because I didn't want to run the risk of getting me ear chewed off for being late. I mean, that would be quite something. To make the wizard cross because I've been early and late in the space of an hour.

Right?

It was still raining, so I huddled close to the buildings on The Pig and Pepper side of the lane, trying to stay dry. If you do it right, it saves you getting wet because the buildings on that side lean more than the others for some reason.

Tudor Lane was quiet. Oddly quiet. But I think that had something to do with the weather, probably. I was almost at The Hat and Dashery and I saw someone come out of the side door. I didn't think anything of it, really. Well, maybe I thought, Oh, that's good. *That means Wizard Dodo is on his own and I can go up.* But apart from that, like, nothing crossed my mind.

And before you ask, because I know you're going to, I didn't see who it was. It was a dark night. He didn't look like more than a dark shadow. He walked straight across to the other side of the lane and melted into the shadows there. I didn't follow him; I didn't even watch him go. He flitted across the lane in front of me and that was the last I saw of him.

This time, I didn't notice whether Hattie's lights were on. The side door wasn't fully closed, so I pushed it open and went on up. I was quiet. I know she doesn't like to be disturbed. The goddess knows she's whinged about it enough in the past. I reached the landing and found the door to the office was ajar. I could see the wizard sitting at his desk.

'Sorry about earlier,' I said and went in. He looked like he'd fallen asleep. Except there was something about his total relaxation that threw me. I'd never seen him like that. I stepped right into the office and called his name.

But he didn't look up.

So I walked over to him and I shook his shoulder.

But I already knew.

I should have called the cops but I panicked! Me

and them and one thing and another ... I just couldn't do it. But I remembered you sitting at the bar and I figured you could help me. I dashed down the stairs and nearly lost my footing on the final flight. I wrenched my wrist catching hold of the banister.

The door was open to the outside and as I waited there a moment—literally just a second or two—just getting my breath and massaging my wrist, I realised someone was watching me from the shadow of the doorway opposite. Just the faintest movement and it caught what limited light there was.

It freaked me out.

I half considered running back upstairs and maybe knocking on Hattie's door, but then I figured there was strength in numbers and The Pig and Pepper would be busier. So I ran out into the lane as fast as I could, and that's when I came to find you ...

I sat back in my chair, the notes in front of me forgotten, studying Snitch's pale face.

Something about his story, the way he had lost himself in his memories of that night, told me he was telling the truth. Over the years I'd taken dozens of statements. I instinctively knew when something sounded honest and heartfelt. Now I fully understood why Snitch had given himself up to the police. He should never have been their chief suspect. If they had only talked to him and dug a little below the surface, they would have realised he was actually their chief witness.

While I couldn't know for certain that the person who had darted out of the building as Snitch arrived just before eleven had been Dodo's killer, there was every possibility he was.

Snitch had been hogging the shadows and not taking much notice of anything, thanks to the lousy weather, but, by the sound of it, the person who had exited the building hadn't gone far. He'd waited to see what Snitch had been up to.

Whether he would discover the body of the dead wizard.

And then he'd loitered in the doorway across the lane, so when Snitch had stumbled down the stairs in a panic, he'd had clear sight of the unfortunate wretch. He would be able to identify Snitch in the future.

And take action if needed.

I blew out a lungful of air.

"You shouldn't be in here," I said.

"It's the safest place I could think of."

"You think that whoever killed Wizard Dodo will come after you?"

He twisted his mouth up, thoroughly miserable.

I nodded in confirmation. I'd been involved in a case a few years ago where a witness to a murder had been finished off before we could apprehend our chief suspect. Intimidation of witnesses was a big problem.

Snitch's pale face had taken on an unmistakable green hue. "If I were a betting man—which I am, as it happens—I'd wager the man in the shadows thinks I saw his face. But I didn't, I swear."

"The problem is, he doesn't know that," I said and closed my notebook.

"Exactly."

"It was definitely a man, was it?" I was thinking we could rule out Hattie as a suspect.

"Oh." Snitch thought for a moment. "I think so."

"*Think* isn't good enough," I reminded him. "I have to deal in conviction. You haven't given me a description to go on."

"It wasn't much more than a shadow. A glimpse."

"You said you heard him talking though."

Now Snitch looked clearer. "That's right." He squinted as he tried to remember. "I recall the words, and I know I had the impression it was a man, so yeah."

I rolled my eyes. It wasn't good enough, but it would have to do for now. "One thing that's been bothering me ..."

Snitch was studying his fingernails again, or what was left of them.

"Given the nature of what you do ..."

He didn't look up but instead became very still.

I cast a hasty glance at the prison officers, but they were engrossed in their own conversation. Nonetheless, I lowered my voice even further. "As a police informant," I said, "it surprises me that you didn't simply go straight to whoever it is who handles you. They know you well enough. They'd take steps to protect—"

"I couldn't." Snitch's voice sounded suddenly harsh. He kept his head lowered but glared up at me. "I only ever dealt with one of your lot, and he's not around anymore."

"Not around? What? Has he retired? Or is he—" As soon as the words were out of my mouth, I realised what he was saying. "Ezra?"

Snitch nodded; his face grim.

"But there's more than that." He leaned forward, his fists clenched together on the table, staring down at them so that he was neither looking at me nor speaking to me directly. I knew what he was doing. If the prison officers looked over, they would not be able to hear him or read his lips.

"There was one of your lot there that night."

I frowned. "Are you sure? Tumble Town's not on our beat. Most of what happens there is handled by the Dark Squad."

"I know that." I could hear a note of frustration entering into Snitch's voice. "But, sure as eggs is eggs, they were there."

"You saw them?"

He shook his head, stealing a glance at me. "I heard them."

"Voices?" I didn't think that would stand up in court. "Were they easy to distinguish? Would you recognise them again if you heard them?"

"I didn't say voices, did I?"

"Go on."

"When I discovered the body, I distinctly heard a police radio. It sounded so close I thought the police had already arrived."

"But there was nobody there."

"I didn't check the back room."

I stared at Snitch in dismay. He met my eyes this time, his face woebegone.

My stomach flipped. If what he was saying were true … "What a murky mess." Perhaps I should reconsider getting involved. "You know what, Snitch? I think you're right. For now, you're better off in here."

I stood up. "Keep your head down. Let me see what else I can find out. Don't talk to anyone else until you hear from me again."

CHAPTER 9

After rescuing my belongings, I fought my way outside through a crowd of women waiting for visiting hours to start. I walked briskly, glad of the fresh air—or fresher air, I suppose I should say—London being a pretty congested city and all that. The magickal conclave that housed the area around Celestial Street and Tumble Town—quite a vast expanse of space to be honest—was less polluted by cars, but Tumble Town itself, with the slums crowded back-to-back and the tall chimneys, both domestic and industrial, that reached up into the sky, well, that was another story.

I bought a cartoon map of Tumble Town from the bookshop used to enter Celestial Street, and made my way to the entrance to Cross Lane, clutching it in my hand. Dusk was a few hours away. If I was going to pay a visit to Wizard Jamendithas Ironhouse, now would probably be a good time to do so.

But first I had to find Clay Court.

I'd enquired of the bookseller, but he'd only looked at me as though I were a bad smell under his nose. "Really madam," he'd said, "I wouldn't know."

In his case, that was probably true. There was a huge amount of snobbery from those who lived on the 'right side' of Cross Lane.

The reverse applied once I'd ventured into Tumble Town proper. There was so much distrust of strangers, that even had I asked anyone whether they knew where Clay Court was, there was no way they'd have told me.

I paused at a crossroads, considering my options. I could venture along to The Pig and Pepper and try and persuade little Wootton to tell me, or further down Tudor Lane, perhaps Hattie would. The sensible thing would have been to ask Snitch this morning.

I stepped back to allow a fully laden mule to pass by and collided with someone coming up behind me. I distinctly heard a crunch, swiftly followed by an 'oof' and a curse. I whirled around.

A postman.

"I beg your pardon!" While he hopped around in agony, I crouched down to retrieve the letters he'd dropped. Fortunately, he hadn't scattered many. "I wasn't looking where I was going." I sensed several pairs of eyes scrutinising us from the shadows—kids on the lookout for some easy pickings, no doubt.

"I gathered that. You've crushed my little toe," he whimpered.

"I am *so* sorry," I said, grimacing. I handed over a pile of letters, along with one small package and a cheap plastic pen.

"Not to worry." He straightened up and stuck the pen behind his ear. "I've got another one on the other foot."

I laughed, relieved he could make a joke out of it. "Sorry again," I said, and he smiled and waved me away.

I began to move, but then it struck me. Of course, a *postie* would know where to find Clay Court.

"Wait!" I called after him. "I realise it's a cheek after I've just assaulted you in such a cruel manner, but would you mind giving me directions?"

He regarded me warily. "Maybe."

I took a step towards him, waving my map.

"Ah-ah!" He stepped away. "Keep away from my toes!"

"Sorry." I held out my map at arm's length. "I'm looking for Clay Court."

He wiggled his eyebrows. "Clay Court, eh?" He

reached for the map, scanned it and then whipped out his pen. "This is not particularly accurate," he told me.

"I bought it from the bookshop." I gestured with my thumb back the way I'd come.

He sniffed. "The bookshop in Celestial Street? Yeah, that's about right. They sell these for tourists."

"Tourists? In Tumble Town?" That was just bizarre.

"Oh, you'd be surprised. Have you never heard of dark tourism?"

"Mmm, nope."

"Look it up." He circled a square and handed it back. "This is the general area. See where I've marked it? That's Peachstone Market. Behind there is Bath Terrace—"

Bath Terrace? Why did that ring a bell?

"—and just to the right of the terrace is a small alley that leads through into Clay Court."

"Smashing, thanks." I smiled at my new friend.

"You want to be careful around there, though," he told me. "Stick to the wider lanes."

"I will," I promised.

"If all else fails, you can cripple any attacker by stepping on their toes," he said. With that, he hurried away to continue with his round, leaving me to navigate further into Tumble Town.

The postman had been right about the map, but as long as you stuck to the main thoroughfares you couldn't go wrong. Woe betide anyone who tried to take a short cut down one of the tiny alleys or lanes that weren't marked on the map. I could see that disaster might befall them. You could get lost and never find your way out—and there would be plenty of the local residents willing to rob you of your belongings and your life, if pushed to it.

I knew how to handle myself on the streets, and in my time I'd taken on some fairly evil beings, but even so, I had a firm grip on my wand and kept my wits about me. You could never know who—or what—was creeping around the corner in these narrow lanes.

Peachstone Market was a pleasant surprise. Arranged in rows covering a large square, there must have been fifty or so stalls. Some were selling fresh fruit and vegetables, meat or fish, others had clothes, but as I cut through to make my way to Bath Terrace I could also see stalls selling gothic jewellery, stalls with wands, others with herbs and vials and ingredients needed for potions, stalls with books and even stalls with animals in cages—cats, birds of the exotic and domestic variety, reptiles, toads and frogs, rabbits and hares and even something that looked like a miniature yak—most of them peering out at shoppers and curious onlookers with a mix of anger and disdain.

The market was a riot of colour, bustling with people, many of whom looked boringly ordinary, rather like myself, but who were probably witches and wizards. There were plenty of odd-bods too, of course, people huddled beneath layers or wrapped in cloaks, faces turned carefully away. Children ran between the stalls or ducked underneath awnings, chasing each other and a bunch of stray dogs.

I found myself next to a water fountain—a large stone structure with a face on each side: a woman, a man, a demon and a goblin. It was slightly disconcerting to watch as water flowed through each of the open mouths. On the step beneath the circular trough, a large furry ginger cat was sitting cleaning its paws. It looked up at me as I passed and, for a second, seemed to smile.

I glanced back at it, but it had disappeared. *Must have walked behind the pillar*, I decided, and carried on.

Bath Terrace was a semi-circle of ten four-storey Georgian buildings. The graceful sweep of their elegant facades, fronted by iron railings, suggested that once upon a time the residents here would have been well-to-do, matching their counterparts who had chosen to live close to Celestial Street, no doubt.

Not so now. The houses here were run down, the stone chipped, the paint peeling, the front doors scuffed and the once-impressive sash windows in desperate need of replacing. I noted as I hooked right, that each of the houses had been converted into apartments. One or two had signs in the downstairs bay window, declaring 'Flat to Let'.

I mentally filed that information away. I didn't think Tumble Town was the place for me, but you never know how desperate you can get. I had rent due on my flat and was going to struggle to keep paying the bills.

"I need to sort my life out," I muttered, searching for the alley that would take me to Clay Court.

And there it was. Where Bath Terrace ended and a line of slightly more modern—as in only two-hundred-year-old—red brick buildings began, there was a passageway. Three feet wide at the most, with a single lamp illuminating the gloom.

I snuck a peek over my shoulder, seeking signs of any obvious threat from behind but seeing none, and ducked into the narrow alley. It ran for around forty yards with impossibly high walls on both sides. It would be the easiest thing in the world to be caught out here. One assailant following, one lying in wait, and a whole heap of trouble.

But I needn't have worried. I slipped along the alley quickly and paused to take in my surroundings.

Clay Court was a revelation. Behind me, tall walls afforded the gardens of Bath Terrace some privacy, but on all three remaining sides, this square of space was composed of identical small, neat, three-storey houses arranged in a horseshoe. Each house had half a dozen steps leading up to the front door, and every individual door had been painted in a brightly coloured gloss. There were iron railings in front of each house, masking steps down to a basement flat. Unlike many areas of Tumble Town, there were containers and hanging baskets, each with bold displays of vibrant flowers.

I realised my head had jutted forwards and my mouth was open, but I had never been aware that areas of Tumble Town could look so ... well ... civilised. I'd seen it only as a dark ghetto, a simmering cauldron of malcontent, a haven for vagabonds.

But perhaps the latter still held true.

I pocketed my wand and reached for my notebook instead.

"Ah ... 3B." I scanned the numbers on the front doors, noting that several of them had brass plaques, presumably indicating the resident had a trade of some kind. The 'B' seemed to refer to the basement flats. I located number 3 Clay Court and headed for the iron railings and the steps down, peering into a window as I passed. A neatly laid out kitchen. The lights were on inside, which was good news.

I tapped the knocker and waited, staring at the mottled glass in the top third of the door. After a few moments, I discerned a shape moving on the other side and heard the scratching sound as the latch was undone.

The door was pulled open by about three inches. A bright green eye with white eyelashes and a bushy eyebrow twitched out at me.

"Jamendithas Ironhouse?" I asked.

Clay Court may have been atypical of Tumble Town, but this occupant clearly wasn't. "Who wants to know?"

"Elise Liddell." I missed the days I'd been able to pull out my warrant card and dazzle any witness or suspect with the bronze of my Ministry of Witches police badge. Hopefully, my official private investigator ID was in the post. "I'm looking into the death of Wizard Dodo."

"It wasn't me."

Interesting response.

"The police have a suspect in custody," I told him, picking my words carefully.

"Do they?" The old fellow pulled the door open a little wider. I could see his long hair now, a kind of iron grey with wispy white bits to match his eyebrows. He wore a long green gown with gold embroidery down the front and a pair of bright red slippers with curly toes. He stopped himself. "Who are *you* if you aren't the police?"

"I'm a private investigator," I told him, trying out the words for the first time. Why did I feel like such a fraud? "Are you Jamendithas Ironhouse?"

"If the police have someone, what's left to investigate?"

Boy, he was a sharp one. I realised that admitting to representing Snitch's interests might not go down well. "I want to get some background on Dodo," I told him. "To help the police out. To make a more rounded case."

He raised his eyebrows. I couldn't tell what he was thinking, but if I was going to ask him any questions, I needed to get him onside. "You are Jamendithas Ironhouse?"

When he shrugged, I decided to try and pander to his vain side. If he had one. "I understand you and he were great friends. You're best placed to tell me more about Dodo."

It worked. He blinked in surprise, any hostility he

may have harboured towards me and my questioning stopped in its tracks.

"Well, yes, we do go way back," he confirmed.

"I thought so." I smiled at him. "I found a few references to you in his diary."

"Dodo kept a diary?"

"Yes," I lied. "It's with the police now, of course."

He swallowed. "Oh."

I found his reaction to my lie curious. What did he imagine Dodo might write about him in a diary?

"Nothing to worry about," I breezed. "As I say, I'm only here to learn more about his background and the sort of man he was. If you have the time, of course." I opened my eyes in what I hoped was wide-eyed innocence.

He shuffled around for a moment, looking out into the courtyard and then behind him at his own house, weighing up his options, no doubt. Eventually he huffed and pulled the door fully open. "Alright. I can spare you ten minutes."

"Thank you." He stood back and, after wiping my feet, I followed him into the small hallway. There was a deep red carpet here—Jamendithas Ironhouse evidently favoured red—and three doors. One of these was closed, while the second led into the living room. Incense wafted out from there and a fire burned in the grate. There were books scattered on the floor as though I had interrupted him in some research.

He opened the third door and indicated I should follow him. This was the kitchen at the front of the property; small but well laid out, with red cupboard doors and red and cream tiles. Even his impressive range was red. I sniffed in appreciation. He'd been baking. The soft and heavenly scent of vanilla and sugar combined made my stomach rumble. He lifted the kettle from the hot plate. "I suppose you'll be wanting tea?"

"That would be lovely, thank you."

He grunted and pointed at a small square wooden table with two mini benches, one on each side. I squeezed into the narrow space, placed my notebook and pen on the table in front of me and my bag on the floor, studying my surroundings. There were no herbs and potions on display, nothing witchy or magickal at all. Not even a pestle and mortar.

He joined me at the table with a tray containing a teapot, a jug of milk and a bowl of sugar, a pair of teaspoons and a plate laden with freshly baked currant fairy cakes, drizzled with pink icing and sprinkled with hundreds and thousands.

My mouth watered.

"You look like you could do with feeding up," he

said. I sensed that, beneath the gruffness, there beat a less than stony heart.

"I appreciate it," I said, wondering how long politeness dictated I should wait before stuffing the first cake in my face. I sat on my hands. "Should I call you Wizard Ironhouse, or—?"

"James," he said, and began to mash the tea.

"Thank you, James." I reached for a bun and carefully pulled the paper case from one part of it, catching the crumbs with my tongue. If you could inhale a cake, I would have done so.

"You can have as many as you like." The wizard regarded me with something akin to amusement in his eyes. "I bake most days."

"Really?" He didn't look like a man who survived on cake and pastry. He had a wiry frame. He might once have been described as athletic.

"I find baking soothes me. I give away a lot of what I make though. To my neighbours." He pointed up at the ceiling, which I took to mean the people in the house above us. "And to the street urchins who run wild in Peachstone Market."

"Do they really run wild?" I asked, concerned at the thought of kids without proper homes.

"Completely feral," James replied. He didn't look concerned.

I finished off the first fairy cake and reached for

another. I hadn't realised how hungry I was. I really should start eating properly.

James nodded at my notebook. "You wanted to know about Dodo?"

"Yes!" I dabbed at the corner of my mouth where a stray crumb had lodged. "You said you went way back?"

He nodded. "We knew each other when we were lads at the local school round here. Corkfields. Do you know it?"

I shook my head and made a note of that, not entirely clear it was pertinent to anything.

"We are—were, I should say—distantly related. I think our grandfathers were cousins or something like that." He waved a hand, dismissing the importance of that relationship. "Then we were at the London Academy of Magick together and shared a flat. That would have been back in the mid-sixties, I suppose. Celestial Street was rocking back then."

"You must have been quite close?" I hadn't attended university myself, but I knew from people who had that those were some of the best days of their lives, and many of the friends they made then would go on to be lifelong buddies.

"We rubbed along. We were never close, if that's what you mean. I had other friends and so did he, so we would hang out with our own crowds and only really meet when the other hogged the bathroom for too long."

"I see."

He lifted the teapot. "I think this is brewed now."

"What did you study?" I asked, accepting the cup he offered me and wondering whether I could take a third cake to go with it.

"My major was in alchemical biofortification. His was in common or garden history of magick. Dull, dull, dull."

"Alchemical ... what?"

"Alchemical biofortification. Basically, breeding crops to increase their nutritional value through the use of transmutation of matter."

"Wow." *Who knew such a thing existed?* "That sounds like important work."

"It is. We have to find a way to feed our increasing populations, don't we?"

I nodded and opted for a third cake after all. It seemed churlish not to. Jamendithas Ironhouse was a feeder in more ways than one.

"So you frowned on Dodo's studies?" I asked. "Is that why your relationship was a little ..."—I considered my word choice carefully—"cool?"

"History is such a waste of time, to my eyes at least. Why look back when you should go forwards?"

I'd always enjoyed history at school, but I let him have

his say. Ezra had always taught me that it was important to open up the conversation with a suspect, not shut it down.

I nodded and he continued, "I mean, how can anyone make a living from studying the history of magick?"

That had never crossed my mind. I supposed they became teachers. Or something. I shrugged. "Wizard Dodo found a way to make a living though."

"Yes, you have to give him that. He was adaptable. He had this idea that too many spells were becoming obsolete, that things are no longer being handed down between father and son and mother and daughter or what have you, in the way that used to happen in the good old days. He was on a mission to save spells from getting lost. He was always on the lookout for spells that he hadn't come across before so—even while he was still a young man—he started collecting spell books and grimoires and letters and what have you."

"And he sold them to make money?"

"He would copy spells and sell them individually, yes."

"There can't have been much money in it," I pondered, more to myself than to him, but James flushed.

"No, there wasn't."

I remembered the pile of unpaid invoices returned

to Dodo. "You would ask him for spells from time to time?"

James had the grace to look shamefaced. He obviously knew where this part of the conversation was heading.

"It was just a joke. I'd ask him for something obscure." He cleared his throat. "You see, he had a flat rate for sending out spells. He didn't charge by the hour for the work he did. I thought that was crazy. I wanted to teach him a lesson."

"So you asked him for spells that you knew would take a long time for him to research—"

He cast down his eyes and gave an almost imperceptible nod of his head.

"—Then he would invoice you and you would refuse to pay."

"It sounds shameful when you say that."

It is shameful, I thought, but with Ezra in my head, I knew I wouldn't articulate such a judgement out loud.

"He would send you reminders, and you would send them back."

James grimaced. "You know about that, do you?"

"He seems to have kept all of his mail dating back years and years. Including those."

James nodded. "I regret it now."

Now that he's dead. "Did you ever fall out about it?"

James wriggled uncomfortably on his bench. "I wouldn't say we fell out. A slight disagreement, possibly."

"Only, you were seen going in the side door—" I couldn't possibly know that Jamendithas was the wizard Hattie had overheard arguing with Dodo on the Sunday afternoon, but I was willing to push my luck.

"The landlady, eh?"

"She told me raised voices were heard on the afternoon of his death."

"We did have a bit of a row," James said, still looking uncomfortable, "but I would never have harmed him. We were like ... brothers."

"The kind of brothers that row and fight," I said.

"And make up afterwards."

We sat in silence. I contemplated the fairy cakes.

Eventually James cleared his throat. "I didn't kill him."

"Where were you late on Sunday night?" I asked.

"I was here, reading and listening to the radio."

"Alone?"

James nodded, his face miserable now. "But it wasn't me, I swear."

"Do you know any reason why anybody would have wanted to harm Dodo?"

He frowned. "Not really. He was a curmudgeonly old so-and-so at times, but harmless enough. I mean, I disparage him and what he did with his life, but think about it"—James leaned across the table, his eyes bright, his eyebrows almost alive—"the amount of knowledge he had about magick and spells that might have otherwise been consigned to history. That's quite something."

In most cases I've worked on, there has never been a lightbulb moment—not like the ones you see detectives on television shows have—but for some reason, James's words lit a spark.

I thought back to the boxes and boxes piled high throughout Dodo's office. The stacks of papers. The pages that had been marked, the inserts between sheets. Who knew what Dodo had uncovered? He'd collected quite a treasure trove.

James had been watching me and now his face paled. "What is it?" he asked. "What are you thinking?"

I stared right back at him, harder than I might normally have. How did I know I could trust him? My natural instinct was never to trust anyone. Particularly wizards and the denizens of Tumble Town. James scored highly on both of those criteria. "Something and nothing, probably."

He lifted the teapot and offered me a top-up but I shook my head.

"You said Dodo had mentioned me in his diary ..." he asked, his voice more tentative.

"I lied." I don't know why I needed to confess that. Perhaps I thought it would further disarm him.

It did. He knocked his cup with the teapot and in an effort to straighten it up, upset the milk jug as well. I hastily grabbed my notebook and pushed my bench backwards to avoid the tidal surge of drips heading my way. He cursed, then, quick as a flash he had his wand out and had hoovered the milk up.

I was impressed.

The table would still need wiping down though.

"You're suddenly very jumpy," I remarked, keeping my tone casual.

He shook his head and pulled himself together. "I didn't hurt him."

I nodded. That seemed the right moment to take my leave. "Thank you for your time and for clarifying a few things."

He followed me to the door, but before I could open it and step outside, he intervened. "Wait. Just one sec!"

I stood in place, one hand on the door, inhaling the musky rose incense that drifted out of the living room. Situated at the rear of the house, it had large patio doors opening out onto the garden beyond. I could see rows and rows of vegetables. Courgettes, runner beans, cabbages, carrot tops, tomatoes. A little oasis hidden from public view in Tumble Town. Before today, I had no idea such a place could exist. This little foray over to the dark side had been eye-opening in any number of ways.

James reappeared clutching a brown paper bag. "Take these with you."

Cakes. I smiled and reached out to take them, but instead of letting go, he snatched at my hand and pulled me closer so that our faces were only inches apart.

"I think you found something," he hissed. "Not a diary, but something else."

"You need to let go of me," I told him, my voice soft.

"If you have what I think you have—"

"I'm not going to ask you again."

He dropped my hand but didn't move away. "Burn it."

I frowned. "What do you mean?"

He reached behind me and I tensed, ready to knock him into oblivion with a swift right thrust to his Adam's apple, but he simply unlocked the door.

"Burn it," he repeated as I stepped out into the stairwell.

"But—"

"You have no idea what you're messing with. And it's not something you want to fall into the wrong hands."

He pulled away.

"How—"

But he'd closed the door in my face, and no matter how hard I knocked, he refused to open it up again.

CHAPTER 10

I returned home to a rent demand and flashing lights on my home phone. I hit play to listen to my messages while I rifled through the contents of my fridge for something vaguely edible that wasn't cake.

One message from my concerned bank manager. Could I contact her to talk about an extension to my overdraft or taking out a loan?

"No," I told the machine, "I can't."

I sniffed the contents of a Tupperware container. It might once have been tuna pasta salad, but it was a one-way trip to dysentery town now.

The second message was from someone asking if I'd ever considered life insurance.

"No," I told the machine, "I haven't."

"Yo, Elise? Are you there? Pick up."

Monkton Wyld.

"Not there? Well, listen. If you get this and you fancy a pie and a pint this evening, I could do with a word. I'll be in The Full Moon. Come and find me, okay?"

Not so long ago I'd have taken that as an order. Now I pursed my lips and rolled my eyes. "Can't a girl have a night in?" I grumbled, but one look at the inch of slimy water in the bottom of my salad drawer made my mind up. I grabbed my bag and my keys and hotfooted it around to Celestial Street.

The Full Moon was a cute old public house not far from the Ministry of Witches. I'd often hung out here with my team in the past. It was a natural haven for coppers who needed a swift detox and a chance to decompress after a heavy day and didn't want to travel far.

The tall, thin building had rooms spread over four floors. The upper rooms had accommodation available —perfect for those staying overnight in London—while on the ground floor there were two bars, one an old saloon style and the other more of a lounge. My preference was for the saloon with its worn benches and colourful cushions, and its jukebox blaring out old classics, but Monkton, being a little more civilised and, I suppose, in need of a chat, had chosen to meet me in the lounge.

"I hope this is your shout tonight," I said as I sidled into the booth opposite my old boss.

"Why would that be any different to any other time we've gone out?" Monkton plucked his glasses away from his face and tilted his head. He had black bags beneath bloodshot eyes. He still looked good, though.

"That's not fair," I told him, "I always pay my way."

"Yeah, right." He beckoned over one of the waiting staff, a cute little faery woman with red hair in complicated braids looped around her head, and freckles that spoke of sunshine and fresh air. I had a sudden yearning to be as far away from smog-ridden, congested London as possible.

"Your usual?" Monkton asked and I nodded. "Chicken and mushroom pie for the lady"—he smirked at me—"and I use that term lightly, and a cheese and potato pie for me."

"Urk. Cheese and potato," I grimaced. "That's a horrible combination."

"What? You don't eat jacket potatoes with cheese?"

"Yeah I do, but—"

"Same thing. What about cheese and onion crisps?"

"Yes, but—"

"There you go. Cheese and potatoes."

"It's completely different!"

He waved a hand at me. "It's *exactly* the same, Liddell."

"Would you like drinks with your order?" the red-headed faery asked.

I'd forgotten she was there. "Blue—" I started to say but stopped myself. "You know what? I'll just have a—" I cast around for a soft drink option and failed to come up with anything that wouldn't have sugar in it. "I'll have a glass of water, please."

"Hoodwinker for me." Monkton waved his pint glass at the faery. She smiled and disappeared. "Are you sick?" he asked, reaching for my wrist to take my pulse.

"No," I told him, yanking my hand away. What was it with men today, pawing at me? "I had the mother of all hangovers the other day and I'm still trying to flush it out of my system."

"Well good for you, I guess. But you know, hair of the dog and all that."

"Absolutely not," I said. "Now, what did you want to see me about?"

"A lack of alcohol is making you grouchy, Liddell."

I groaned and sank back into my seat. The booths in The Full Moon were far too comfortable. I'd fallen asleep in here on more than one occasion. "I'm just tired."

"I had a request for a reference for you today."

Ah. That's what this was about.

"I thought you were going to come back to us." Monkton wasn't pleading. Not exactly. But there was something in his eyes.

"I never said I would do that."

"You were considering a sabbatical. That was my understanding."

"I didn't promise that, though."

Monkton screwed up his face. "You really want to go it alone?"

How could I explain how I felt? Losing Ezra was something I'd never get over. I didn't want to have to go through anything like that again. Ever. "Yes."

"A private investigator though?" I could hear the disbelief in his voice, and something else. Disdain?

"It makes sense." I guarded my tone, maintaining icy neutrality. "I have the necessary skills."

"But you won't have the same authority you had as a police officer."

The man was like a dog with a bone; he wouldn't let it rest. What business was it of his?

"I'll have a licence to practise," I reminded him, "assuming you give me a reference. And I'm perfectly capable of making citizen's arrests. I'm no shrinking violet."

"I know that," he soothed, backtracking hastily.

We stared each other out until at last he gave in. "I'm sorry. It was a bit of a shock."

"I suppose it was." I grudgingly accepted his apology. "To be honest, it was a spur of the moment decision."

"Well, there you are then!" Monkton sounded hopeful.

I crushed that hope with a well-placed heel. "That I'm completely comfortable with."

The red-headed faery appeared at the table with our drinks, arranged them on beermats and floated away again.

"Fair enough," he said, watching her depart. "Get it?" He jerked his head after the departing figure. "Faery Nuff."

"Enough with the dad jokes," I said, but I had to giggle.

"What prompted this sudden move?" he asked, relaxing as I let down my guard.

"The Dodo case." I dipped my finger into my glass, making the ice and lemon bob up and down. "It's an intriguing one."

"Is it?" He looked blank. "I'm pretty much hands-off on it." That's the way he worked. He had numerous detective inspectors working under him, and each of those had their own caseload and own team. He kept an overview of everything, though. I'd always felt he had his finger on the pulse of each case I'd worked on.

"I thought we had somebody for it." He lifted his pint to take a gulp.

"You do," I told him. "My client."

He swallowed hastily and stared at me in horror. "You already have a client? Crikey! You move fast."

"I have a reputation to build."

"Are you trying to get him off the hook?"

"I don't need to get him off the hook for a murder he didn't commit. He didn't do it. I want the real culprit caught."

"I'm not aware there are any other suspects." Monkton frowned, evidently trying to recall what he knew about the case. Not as much as I'd hoped, evidently.

Our dinner arrived at that moment and I sat back to stare at the steaming plate. A good-size chicken pie with thick rough puff pastry, a large dollop of mashed potato, buttery cabbage and a tureen of chicken gravy.

Monkton had the same but with a cheese, potato and onion pie and vegetable gravy. I had to admit, his looked equally tasty.

When the faery had gone and I'd taken the first

few bites of my heavenly pie, a sudden thought occurred to me.

"Can I ask you something?"

"You're obviously going to," Monkton said, blowing on a forkful of steaming melted cheese and potato.

"Do you have another police operation going on in Tudor Lane?"

"In Tumble Town?" Monkton regarded his fork with happy longing.

"Yes, Tudor Lane in Tumble Town."

He shovelled the pie into his mouth, forcing me to wait while he navigated the fire on his palate. He gasped and took another swig of his beer. "Oooh! That's hot!" he said eventually, when he could speak again. "Not as far as I know. But it seems unlikely. You know we don't tend to take on cases over there."

"You leave it to the Dark Squad, I know." I chewed thoughtfully on my cabbage. "Would you be able to find out for me, do you think?"

Monkton blinked at me. "Hang about—"

"I know, I know." I held my cutlery up to ward off his protests. "I know what you're going to say, but we're on the same side, right?"

"When did I start working for you?"

"We're co-operating," I told him. "In the interests of justice."

"Is that what it is?"

"It is."

He tutted and returned to his pie. I left him in peace for a few mouthfuls but eventually, I couldn't resist. "So, will you?"

"What? Work for you?"

"*With* me," I replied, trying my best to remain patient with him. "Find out whether there were any police officers of any kind operating in Tudor Lane on Sunday evening."

"Leave it with me," he said.

CHAPTER 11

The following day did not start well.

The apartment above mine was having 'work done'. I couldn't tell you whether it was a kitchen or a bathroom, but it sounded as though the ceiling was about to come down on top of me. Perched at my dining table with a mug of black coffee—my milk had turned sour—trying to read through my notes, I glowered up at the ceiling in loathing.

The only positive takeaway from the situation was that I didn't have a hangover. I thanked the goddess for giving me the strength to lay off the Blue Goblin, at least temporarily.

When the frenetic banging and crashing and the sound of breaking tiles became too much for me, I packed up my notebook, my laptop and some pens and headed downstairs for the communal entrance.

Unfortunately for me, Marian, the landlady was loitering there, watching the builders coming in and out with beady black eyes and a permanent scowl of disapproval.

I tried to sneak past her while she was repri-manding some perplexed young man for scratching the paintwork on the first-floor landing—he hadn't; it had been that way since I'd moved in, and I knew that because it had been my removal firm that had done it— but she darted out her hand and clamped her fingers around my bicep. Marian was only a small woman, but she was as strong as an ox. I turned back to meet her glittering gaze.

"Miz Liddell?"

She'd always refused point-blank to use my DI title, but she usually called me by my first name at least. I figured if she was resorting to my last name, I was in trouble.

"Hey, Marian. How're you doing?" I smiled, hoping to charm her.

It didn't work. She cut straight to the chase. "You're overdue." She meant my rent, of course.

"Sorry about that, Marian. I've had a little issue with my bank." *And the lack of money therein.* "I'm sorting it, don't worry—"

"I'm not worried." She pulled a face and raised her shoulders to her ears. "Why would I worry? I have a waiting list of folk wanting to move in here. This is a des res, right?"

"It is. Absolutely." My stomach sank. What could I tell her? I couldn't pay. Try as I might, I couldn't conjure money I didn't have.

"I treat my tenants well, as you know."

"You do," I agreed, feeling increasingly miserable.

"And now I'm refurbishing several of the flats—"

"Smashing! They'll look wonderful."

"But of course, I need to reconsider the favourable rents I charge."

That was all I needed. "The thing is, Marian"—I hesitated, shocking myself with what I knew I was about to say—"I'm moving out."

"You are?" She raised her eyebrows. "You found somewhere else to go?"

"Yes," I lied.

"But the rent you owe—"

"I'll pay it." *Somehow.* "I need to dash. Sorry!"

I pushed my way through the front door, nearly knocking the young builder off his feet in my rush to get away.

"You'd better!" Marian shouted after me.

I waved without looking back and hurried away from her angst.

"Would you like some more coffee?"

I looked up from my screen. I'd been taking advantage of the free Wi-Fi connection at The Pig and Pepper for a good hour, lingering over a long-cold cup of coffee.

Wootton waggled his coffee pot over my mug.

"No," I told him, "I'd better not." I knew how much money I had in my purse. Or didn't have. What was there had to last.

"It's on the house." Before I could protest, he had filled my mug to the brim. "If you want a vodka, you'll have to pay for it though."

I grinned. "What does the landlord think of you giving away free coffee?" I asked.

He shrugged. "What he doesn't know won't hurt him." He edged out the chair next to mine with his foot and took a seat. "Honestly, he makes a mint on this place."

"Does he?" I looked around doubtfully. It never seemed that busy whenever I visited. Ironically, that's why I liked it. I wouldn't be hit on by desperate men looking for a good time. Something they were unlikely to get in my company. This morning, I'd figured the pub would be quieter than my flat.

"Yeah, he does. He waters down the beer and pays the staff peanuts. Trust me. He's doing fine."

Wootton met my eyes. I studied his face. He had

pixie features, I realised. Slightly curved eyes curling upwards, a slight point to the ears, a thin nose. But he was handsome. Porcelain skin and white, even teeth, dark floppy hair and the makings of a beard.

And far too young for me.

"Are you chatting me up?" I came straight to the point.

He gasped. I couldn't decide whether that was out of genuine shock or whether he was putting it on. "Hell no, Grandma."

It was my turn to be taken aback. "I'm not *that* old!"

"Not far off." He crooked an eyebrow at me. "No point in faux outrage."

"You cheeky monkey!" I stared at him, agog at his nerve.

He chortled and all of a sudden, we were laughing together. I narrowed my eyes at him. "Just watch it," I muttered.

"I'm Wootton." He held out his hand and I shook it.

"Elise Liddell."

"What are you doing?" He leaned over to read my notes. "Shopping?"

Closing my notebook, I affected an air of superiority. "None of your business."

He cocked his head to get a better look at my computer screen. "Knives?"

I slapped the lid of the laptop down. "Do you mind?"

"You're not shopping for knives. You're investigating Wizard Dodo's murder, right?" His voice, a little loud, carried through the quiet pub.

Out of habit, I looked around, wanting to see if anyone was listening. "Keep your voice down," I hissed.

"Why?" he wanted to know. "Is it a secret?"

"It's not a secret. I just don't want everyone to know."

"Ah, gotcha." He reached out to pull my notebook towards him. "I'm good at murder mysteries. I could help."

I slapped at his hand. "What do you mean, you're good at murder mysteries?"

"Like detective stories. Books. Movies. Television. I've watched all the CSI re-runs on Witchflix. And Morse. That's my favourite. Oh!" He shot a finger into the air. "And Midsomer Murders. I love those."

"Hmpf." I rolled my eyes. "Believe me, real-life murder is nothing like—"

"Oh, I know, I know." He laughed. "But I can always solve the ones on TV."

"Well, good for you." I gave him a pointed look, hoping he'd take the hint and leave me alone.

He jumped up. "Hey! I found something this morning you might be interested in."

"Really?" I couldn't help the sarcasm. I could barely rein in my enthusiasm. What could Wootton possibly have found that would help me?

"One sec!" He darted away and disappeared behind the bar. A few seconds later, he reappeared clutching a newspaper.

"How does this help me?" I asked as Wootton threw himself back into the seat next to me.

"It's an article that *The Celestine Times* ran a week ago. I found it this morning when I was laying the fire ready to light. It was about The Hat and Dashery; Hattie's exceptionally good at courting publicity. But while they were there, they interviewed Wizard Dodo, too." Wootton lay out the newspaper in front of me. One and a half colourful pages had been devoted to Hattie and her marvellous creations. He tapped a photograph on the left-hand page contained within a boxed section. Wizard Dodo, sitting at his desk, not smiling, surrounded by clutter.

"They could at least have tidied the desk up," I said, studying the range of paraphernalia. The mugs, the pens, the stress ball, the letter opener, the—

"A letter opener." I plucked up the newspaper and squinted to get a better look.

A thin blade with a blue, marbled handle. I hadn't seen it on the desk on the night of the murder. It hadn't been in the boxes packed up by the police ready to ship back to the department. Monkton hadn't mentioned finding it.

"So where did that go?" I wondered.

"Is the newspaper useful?" Wootton beamed at me.

"It may well be." I allowed my thoughts to churn away for a minute. Potentially, if this was the murder weapon, it proved the killing wasn't premeditated. The murderer had acted on impulse for some reason. It didn't rule out Hattie or Snitch, but at least, if it could be located, it might lead us to the perpetrator.

That was a big if.

"May I keep this?" I asked Wootton.

He looked thrilled. "Absolutely!"

"Thanks." I smiled at him.

"I'd better get back to work."

He pushed his chair back, but we were interrupted before he could stand.

"Hey, Wootton. What you up to, man?" A large biker with a bushy black beard, a shaved head and forearms full of tattoos approached us.

"I'm just helping DI Liddell here with her murder investigation."

The biker shot me a look. I knew that look. He was clocking me for future reference. Way to go, Wootton.

I began to gather my things together. It looked like The Pig and Pepper wasn't a good place for me to work either.

"Can I get a beer, man?" the biker asked, but he didn't take his eyes from me.

"Hey absolutely, *man*." Wootton imitated his drawl. "I'll bring it over." The biker nodded and walked away.

Wootton leaned in towards me and offered me his most engaging smile. "Seriously? If you ever need an assistant, I'm your guy. I'll work for slightly more peanuts than they pay here."

"I'll bear that in mind." I pushed my chair backwards, stood and picked up my belongings. "Thanks for the coffee."

Wootton leapt up with me and bowed flamboyantly as I started for the exit. "See you soon, Grandma!" he called after me.

It was just after midday. I didn't want to go back to my apartment—I wouldn't have been able to work there anyway—and working at The Pig and Pepper was out of the question, along with the other pubs and taverns sprinkled around Tumble Town. I didn't want to run the risk of anyone else snooping over my shoulder. At the moment I didn't really know what I was dealing with. It wasn't worth the risk.

I stood in Tudor Lane, puffing my cheeks out and pondering whether a trip to the library was a good idea or not. Just at that moment a fat blob of rain fell on the top of my head. Within seconds, one fat blob had become multiple fat blobs as the heavens opened.

A little way up the cobbled street, a hanging shop sign caught a sudden breeze and squeaked on its rusty hinges. The Hat and Dashery. I stared at the iron sign, depicting the Mad Hatter from Alice in Wonderland holding a cup and saucer. The soft glow from the shop window told me Hattie was busy at work. I decided to pay her a visit, maybe ask her a few more questions, but primarily seek shelter from the downpour.

I ran up the lane, my shoes slipping on the wet cobbles, and had almost reached the shop door when the side door opened and DC Pritchard stepped out, shaking her umbrella loose.

"Hey!" I said.

"Hey yourself." Cerys smiled at me as her umbrella opened with a pleasing whoosh, not unlike the sound a parachute makes when the cord is pulled and the canopy opens.

"I thought you'd be finished by now." I pointed upwards.

"Yeah, yeah, we are. I was just ... finalising things."

"Do you have all the information you need?" Really, I was only making conversation.

"Pretty much. Everything's been boxed up and collected."

That surprised me. There had been a huge number of boxes. "Really? Already? You're storing everything at HQ?"

She picked at a thread hanging from the inside of her umbrella. "It has to be stored somewhere."

"That's true!" *If everything had been collected, what was she doing here?* "Were you looking for something in particular?"

"Now that would be telling." She winked and laughed, her tone light. "You know I can't get into details with you anymore, Elise."

"No, of course. I understand." My eyebrows were becoming saturated by the rain. I needed to get indoors.

"What are *you* doing here?" she asked. Was that suspicion I heard in her voice or merely curiosity?

"I thought I'd pop in and see Hattie."

"I didn't know you two were friends."

I decided to lie. "We go way back." All the way to

last Sunday, in fact. "The Pig and Pepper is virtually a second home." I jerked my head down the lane.

"I didn't know that," Cerys said.

"Mm. No reason why you should." I had a sudden thought. "You must have had your ear to the ground around these parts lately."

"You're not wrong. I might as well have taken up residence."

"You haven't heard whether there are any other investigations taking place hereabouts, have you?" Monkton hadn't come back to me and I wondered whether Cerys, given that she worked here at the coal-face, so to speak, might be better informed.

She shook her head. "No, not to my knowledge. Are you thinking of anything specific? A break-in? Mugging?"

"To be honest, I have no idea. It's a shot in the dark. I have a source that suggests there was some police activity in Tudor Lane on the day that Wizard Dodo was murdered."

"Is that right?" Cerys stared at me, her face blank. "A source?"

"Yes." I waited. I wasn't about to snitch on Snitch.

"Nope. Can't say I've heard that. I should look into it though. They might have noticed something untoward."

"Exactly." I nodded. "But it could be something

and nothing, you know?"

"You're probably right."

We stood awkwardly for a moment.

I broke the silence. "We must arrange for that coffee sometime. I'll call you."

She looked relieved, as though I'd suddenly given her permission to leave a tense meeting or something. "Do that!" she enthused. "Right. I'd best get off."

She twitched her umbrella at me, loosening a shower of droplets, and hurried away. I stood for a moment, watching her go. When the rain began to plaster my hair against my head, I made a dash for Hattie's doorway.

"You're very damp!" Hattie had a customer, but she grabbed a tea towel and offered it to me. "Careful you don't drip on my hats."

"Sorry." I hastily dabbed at the worst of the drops. Hattie's male customer, sitting on a stool, with his little feet dangling well off the floor, was trying on a tall top hat, the chimney of it nearly two feet in height. Hattie had been decorating it with an assortment of felted fruit. "I didn't realise you were busy. I was trying to work in the pub but kept being interrupted."

Hattie snorted. "I shouldn't have thought that

would be a particularly calm environment." She indicated the hat. "What do you think?"

"It's incredible," I said. "It's so ... tall."

The little man beamed. "I'm trying to make up for my limited stature."

"You'll undoubtedly succeed in that," I nodded. "But will you be able to walk in it?"

"Of course he will!" Hattie blustered, and gave me a stern look. "It's a good job you're not after a job selling hats."

"If it was paying, I think I'd take anything at the moment." I shrugged. "I'm sorry," I apologised again. "I can see you're busy. I'll catch up with you again soon."

I turned for the door, but Hattie called me back. "Wait!" She rummaged in her desk drawer for her key. "If you're looking for somewhere quiet out of the rain to work for a few hours, why not do it in Dodo's office?"

"Are you sure?"

"Absolutely. It's no use to him anymore, is it?" She blinked away the sudden moisture from her eyes. "He's not there."

I pushed open the door to Wizard Dodo's office and raised my eyebrows. Cerys hadn't been lying when she said everything had been collected.

She'd meant *absolutely* everything. Every box, every book, every piece of paper, the printer, the contents of every drawer—right down to the last stray paperclip.

"Wow."

All that remained were the desk, a couple of chairs, the bookshelves, a few wilting pot plants and the kitchen items. Now that the room had been cleared, I could see how filthy it was. The thin carpet had probably been down since the seventies, the paintwork was mottled with damp patches. There was dust everywhere, creating outlines where Dodo's possessions had previously lived. The room felt cold and sad.

I dumped my bag on the desk and, with one eye on the open door, knelt on the worn carpet until I could see where I'd found the key previously. Still there. Although I'd kept the little notebook, I'd returned the key to its hiding place. A quick scout in the drawer showed me that no-one had found the secret cubbyhole there.

I stood up. Some of my ex-colleagues needed a refresher's course in searching a crime scene.

With the exception of the rain drumming on the roof and dripping from the guttering outside—somehow soothing—everything was quiet. I'd be able to work here, but first I decided to wipe the desk down; there was fingerprint dusting powder everywhere.

I wandered into the back room. There were a few cleaning materials under the sink, including a well-used cloth and a bottle of washing-up liquid. I ran the water into the sink until it was warm, added some bubbles and rinsed the cloth through before going back into the main room and wiping the desk and chair down thoroughly. While I was at it, I watered the plants. I could almost hear them sigh with relief.

Then I sat down at the desk, pulled open my laptop and my notebook and began to think.

"You look right at home there."

I glanced up from the diagram I'd been drawing. In the absence of a whiteboard, I'd had to do it old school, doodling across two facing pages of my notebook, neatly boxing in names, highlighting potential motives, drawing arrows between people as I attempted to ascertain relationships.

Hattie stood at the top of the stairs with a cardboard tray from Betty's Bakery. "I thought I'd return the favour from the other day."

"How lovely! Thank you!" I indicated the chair opposite me and closed my notebook.

"Have you dried off?"

I felt my hair. Still damp. "Just about."

"You've managed to do some work?" She prised the lid from one of the cardboard cups and peered in. "Coffee. That's yours. Hope that's okay."

"Perfect."

"And a pasty. I thought you might want a spot of lunch, and Betty's do make the most amazing pasties. A genuine West Country recipe, I believe."

"I do love a pasty," I said, and it was true, although they reminded me of my visit to Whittle Inn and losing Ezra. I shook that thought out of my mind and took the paper package that Hattie offered.

Hattie fished out a teabag from her cup. "I prefer tea from a teapot, but I didn't want to risk climbing those stairs with a tray full of china." She looked around. "It's very odd without all of Wizard Dodo's stuff in here."

"It is," I agreed. "It's much bigger than it seemed when all his books were strewn around."

"Do you think he died during a burglary?" Hattie asked.

I broke off a chunk of pastry from the corner of my pasty. The knob. That was my favourite bit. "I don't suppose anything has been ruled out." I chewed for a moment, thinking about what she'd said. It would be a robbery rather than a burglary, but not many people know the difference. "Why do you ask that? There hasn't been any indication of—"

"Just that it was all rather a mess when he was found, wasn't it?"

I couldn't hide my surprise. "Messier than normal?" I hadn't for a moment assumed that the office had been ransacked.

Hattie waved a hand around the empty room. "Oh yes, he was chaotic at times, but there was a kind of order to it all. He did have piles of things everywhere, but that was his filing system. He was actually incredibly careful about where he stored things."

And you're telling me this now?

I stared at Hattie through the steam rising from my coffee. Was she just saying this to put me off the scent? Instinctively, I rather liked her, as eccentric as she was, but one should never let one's feelings get in the way of the pursuit of justice.

"How did he remember where everything was?" I asked. "He was dealing with a phenomenal amount of information. Did he keep an index anywhere? On his computer?"

Hattie laughed. "I don't think he kept it on his computer, although he might have done. He didn't really like computers. He always said they would put people like him out of business."

"He must have had some sort of catalogue," I mused. "He couldn't have stored it all in his own memory."

"You're right there," Hattie agreed. "He had a terrible memory. He was forever losing his keys and his wand or forgetting to go to the post office. That's why he liked having Bartholomew around, I think."

"Did Bartholomew hang around a lot?" I asked.

"Quite a lot. Always at a loose end, I suppose."

"And to the best of your knowledge, did Wizard Dodo have anything worth stealing? Anything valuable?"

"I doubt it. He could barely scrape his rent together most months."

I lapsed into silence. *What did Dodo have that someone else might want? Not money. Nor possessions.*

Hattie let me ruminate for a while, silently sipping her tea and appraising me.

Eventually she spoke up again. "Just a thought, but if you ever want an office ..."

"Hmmm?" I came back to reality.

"I was just saying, if you ever want an office, I'll be looking to let this out again soon."

An office! I needed an office!
But in Tumble Town?

I caught my breath in excitement, thinking rapidly. Did I want to be based in Tumble Town? Well, why not? I needed to be somewhere among potential clients. It would be all well and good renting a space in Celestial Street or somewhere around there, but the rent would be extortionate. Here in Tumble Town, rent would be cheaper … and … thinking about it, clients more plentiful. I'd be surrounded by rogues and rascals.

It would be perfect.

"Yes! I need an office!" The words tumbled out in a rush. "But how much?" I grimaced at Hattie. "I'm a little strapped for cash at the moment."

"Isn't it always the way?" Hattie laughed and replaced the cap on her tea. I noticed she hadn't touched her pasty. "We'll work something out. Truth to tell, I like the idea of having an ex-copper up here. Makes me feel a little more secure." She slid her pasty across the desk towards me. "Take this. Have it for your dinner."

I was touched by her generosity. "I will pay you," I promised.

"I know." She winked at me and turned for the door. "Keep the key. You'll have to clean the place up yourself."

"No problem," I said. "Thank you!" I called as she descended the stairs.

"No callers after ten in the evening," she shot back at me as she disappeared from view.

I sat back in my chair and stared around the space. *My* space!

My detective agency had a base!

CHAPTER 12

"**D**id you find out who killed me yet?"

I shot upright and blinked. Dozing off at the desk in Dodo's office—sorry, *my* office—was turning into a habit. It was dark outside; the rain still coming down. It had been those gentle sounds that had lulled me to sleep. I checked the time. Just after nine. Not even that late. But my eyes were gritty, my head sluggish and my throat parched.

"Ugh." I swallowed, yawned and stretched, staring out onto the dark landing. Nobody there. Nobody in the office. I must have been having a dream.

"The place to have dreams is in your own bed," I said, standing and walking to the door to close it. Thinking of my comfortable bed, with a thick feather duvet and squidgy pillows, reminded me that for some strange reason, I'd handed in my notice to Marian.

"What was I thinking?" I could at least have waited until I had a better idea of where I could move to. I looked around the office. What about this place? It wouldn't do in the long run, especially if I wanted to operate my business from here, but I supposed if Hattie wouldn't mind, I could crash on the floor while I got myself sorted out. My belongings would just have to go into storage for a while.

I sat down at the desk again, not with the intention of doing any more work but to clear everything up. I stared down at the notes and charts and diagrams I'd been drawing. I'd been doing a little digging on Bartholomew, Hattie and Jamendithas Ironside, but hadn't uncovered anything particularly derogatory about any of them. Jamendithas in particular had a good reputation as an academic and researcher, but I couldn't shake the thought that there was more to him than met the eye.

I shuffled the papers together and capped my pens. I might as well leave everything here on the desk and return in the morning.

"Did you find out who killed me yet?"

I jumped a mile and spun around in my seat. "Who's there?"

"What do you mean, who's there?"

I stood, slowly, craning my neck to peer into the darkened back room. "Hello?"

"Are you completely blind? I'm here! I'm standing right in front of you!"

I caught my breath, my muscles freezing. My eyes swivelled in their sockets, left to right and back again. "What?"

"May the goddess help me. I'm here! I'm right here!" Whoever it was, they sounded annoyed now.

I stretched my hands out. There was nothing in front of me. I wasn't crazy.

"Wait." The voice sounded suddenly suspicious. "Are you one of those very short-sighted people?"

"No." I flapped at the air. "I just can't see you. Are you a ghost?"

"By Jove. You've hit the nail on the head there, my girl."

"There's no need for sarcasm," I told the jeering voice. "I can't see you. I thought ghosts could be seen, albeit a bit translucent or something." I recalled the ghosts at Whittle Inn. They were all readily apparent.

"You can't see me at all?" Now the voice sounded disappointed. "Oh, that's regrettable. I was hoping to start a new career haunting all the people who never paid their bills."

"Wizard Dodo?"

"Indeed. Who else would it be?"

Perplexed, I gazed around the empty office, unclear about what I expected to see. "I suppose you could still haunt people," I suggested. "I mean, it's fairly disconcerting to have a disembodied voice chatting to you."

"Is that what we're doing?" I sensed his disapproval. "Chatting?"

"We could cut to the chase." I rummaged on my desk for my notebook and flipped it open on the diagram I'd made with a list of potential suspects. "Why don't you tell me who killed you?"

"Oh." Now he sounded devastated. "I was hoping you could tell me."

"You don't remember?"

"No." He sniffed. "Don't you know?"

"Are you pulling my leg? I'm scrabbling around trying to find out, but I don't have many clues. *You* were there! How come you don't recall what happened?"

"I don't know. My memory is a blank."

"That's just not helpful." I dropped my notebook on the desk. "What's the last thing you can remember?"

"Lunch."

"Lunch? Okay. That's a start. We're only missing ten hours or so, but it's helpful. We can take it from there." I wondered how admissible evidence from a ghost would be in court. I decided to cross that particular rainbow bridge when I came to it.

"I had slow-cooked brisket of beef with swede and carrot mash, my absolute favourite."

"Is that right?" I had a feeling it couldn't be. "What time did you finish your lunch?

"Around half two or so."

"No, you can't have." I reached for my notebook again. "According to what Bartholomew Rich told me, you had something from the bakery. He walked back from there with you and you arranged to see him a little later."

Wizard Dodo was having none of it. "My final memory is of Sunday lunch at The Nautical Mile."

"Oh." I closed my eyes for a second. We were talking at cross purposes.

That was the last thing he remembered, but it hadn't happened on his last day. We weren't missing ten hours, we were missing at least seven days, but that depended which Sunday he was referring to. We might have been missing weeks!

"Who did you meet at The Nautical Mile?" I asked, on the off chance we were only talking about a few hours' difference.

There was silence.

"Wizard Dodo?" I prompted.

More silence. The rain spattered against the window.

"Are you still there?"

I'd just about given up when the wizard spoke again. "I can't recall." His voice sounded weedy, further away. "I'm sorry."

I felt a pang of compassion for him. It can't be easy to be murdered, then discover your ghost has no form and realise that you've lost key parts of your memory. "Don't worry!" I replied, keeping my voice breezy. "I'll work with that and report back."

I waited for him to respond but he didn't.

It was like he'd never been there at all and I'd been talking to myself.

I stood under The Hat and Dashery's canopy watching the raindrops bounce off the cobbles. They shone in the light spilling out from the shop. I could see Hattie hard at work inside, sewing a bunch of felt grapes to the enormous chimneyed top hat, at her work desk. I decided not to disturb her but to head straight home.

The problem was, I didn't have an umbrella with me. I was dithering under the shop canopy and avoiding the wet weather, even while knowing it wasn't about to ease off and, one way or another, I was going to get soaked on my way home.

"There'll be a hot bath at the end of it," I muttered to myself, and, while I'd forgotten to pick up milk or any provisions today, at least I had Hattie's pasty tucked away in my bag.

I'd just about summoned the willpower to start for home when my phone began to vibrate in my pocket. I plucked it out and thumbed the screen. Monkton.

As my phone connected, I heard the roar of voices in the background and some excited presenter shrieking about a penalty. Evidently Monkton was in a bar watching football somewhere.

"Hi," I said.

Static, then, "Hi."

"Hello? I can hardly hear you."

"Hang about, let me just ..." I heard shuffling and the cacophony in the background cut off as though someone had muted the sound on a television. "I've come outside. Is that better? Can you hear me now?"

"Perfectly. Where are you?"

"My local. Not long finished work. Thought I'd pop in for a quick pint. Forgot England were playing tonight. It's rammed in there."

Football. Eww.

"Do you have any news for me?" I deliberately steered the conversation away from how England was doing. I didn't want to know. It was rarely good news.

"I do, as it happens. I had a look at the case logs for the Sunday evening and until your call, registered at sixteen minutes past midnight on Monday, we hadn't received anything from Tumble Town at all in twenty-four hours."

"Right." I frowned.

"Now that isn't unusual," Monkton continued. "As a rule, the Dark Squad attends all serious incidents on that side, but—"

I pricked my ears up.

"Just to verify that info, I looked at officer logs for Sunday evening and we did have a pair of officers in the general vicinity. They claimed to be pursuing a suspect."

"Did they bring a suspect in that evening?"

"Nothing on the arrest sheet. I enquired of the duty custody sergeant. She told me that the first person to come in with a Tumble Town address after the murder was—"

"Bartholomew Rich on Monday morning," I finished for him.

"Bingo."

"Who were the officers who claimed to be pursuing a suspect?" I asked. "Maybe I could talk to them and see if they spotted anyone in Tudor Lane that night. Throw the search a little wider."

"You've already spoken to them, I expect. DC Cerys Pritchard and her partner DC Kevin Makepeace."

I felt stung. Cerys and I were friends. Why hadn't

she mentioned to me she was out and about in Tumble Town on the night of the murder?

"I don't think I've helped very much, have I?" There was an indistinct collective groan in the background at Monkton's end. Monkton tutted. "Blast. By the sound of it, Spain have equalised."

Fascinating.

Not.

"Thanks for the information," I said. "Get back to the game." I could tell he was dying to. And anyway, I needed to process what he'd just told me. "I'll speak to you soon."

"Take care."

"You too."

By the time I arrived home, I was soaked through to the skin, and my clothes and bag were sopping wet. Even my boots squelched as I walked. I kicked them off and left them outside the door of my apartment. If one of my neighbours wanted to walk off with them, fine. The insides would stink to high heaven by the morning and I couldn't imagine I'd ever wear them again.

After grabbing a towel and swiping at my dripping hair, I rescued the contents of my bag, dumping everything on the dining room table and spreading the items out so the air could get to them. Fortunately, I'd left my laptop and notebooks in Dodo's office—and yes, I really needed to start thinking of it as *my* office—so it was only my personal belongings that had become water-logged. My biggest worry was Hattie's pasty.

And Dodo's notebook!

I picked it up and examined it, a little damp and ragged around the edges, but having been sandwiched between a bunch of envelopes and my purse, it had survived. I flicked through the pages, imagining the ink running, but there was still nothing to see.

I couldn't stop puzzling why Cerys had omitted telling me about being in the vicinity of Tudor Lane on the night of the murder. We were friends. She had no need to be evasive. And ... thinking about it ... what had she been doing in Dodo's office when I'd caught her there earlier today?

She'd claimed to be 'finishing up', but the only things left in the office had been a couple of half-dead plants and piles of dust. Had she been looking for something?

"This notebook." I turned it over and over in my hands. So *ordinary*.

Apart from the fact that it was well-thumbed and yet ... empty.

"You're definitely hiding secrets of some kind," I told it.

I stroked the cover. A magickal notebook? That was feasible. If it wouldn't talk to me, who would it communicate with? I should have asked Dodo's ghost. I half considered heading back out to The Hat and Dashery, but the rattle of my windows reminded me why that wouldn't be a good idea. Not tonight.

I'd have to wait till morning.

My phone began to ring. Not my mobile. The landline. I half considered letting the answer machine pick up but once a police officer, always a police officer. You never knew how urgent a call might be.

I wandered over and glanced at the display. My mother. I picked up.

"Hi Mum."

"Lees?" She sounded surprised.

Who else would it be? She'd called me, after all. Perhaps she'd meant to phone one of my siblings.

"Yeah, 'lo." I automatically lapsed into my thirteen-year-old self.

"How are you?" she asked. "I haven't heard from you for ages." Her words were slightly slurred. She liked a drink in the evening. Maybe a little too much. That's probably where I'd picked up the habit. Or maybe that was just a rubbish excuse on my part. Whatever. I knew she was lonely; she had been since my father had passed away. I tried not to think about it.

I felt guilty enough about not spending enough time with her as it was.

"I'm fine, Mum. How are you?" I asked gently.

"Oh, you know." She sighed in a way that told me she wasn't.

"How's work?" She worked in the Witch Civil Service. Although she was looking forward to retirement, she was still only in her late fifties so had a while to wait yet.

"Great!" She sounded a little more enthusiastic now. "They gave me a pay rise!"

"Brilliant!" I smiled. "Not before time."

"What about you? Did you make any decisions yet?"

I took a deep breath. How would what I was about to say would pan out? She and Dad had always been so proud of me working for the Ministry of Witches Police Department. I think they'd imagined I'd go far. Hell, *I* had imagined I would go far.

"I decided to quit," I told her and waited for an explosion. None came.

"Probably for the best," she said, and her tone was mild. "It had started to stress you out far too much."

"It had." I couldn't disagree.

"And without that nice man you worked with—"

"Ezra," I reminded her.

"Yes, Ezra, sorry. Lovely man. Without him, I would have worried about you."

"He always had my back," I agreed, flopping down on the sofa.

"So, what are you planning on doing now?" She sounded genuinely curious. Maybe not quite three sheets to the wind, after all.

"I'm going it alone," I told her, tucking my feet under me. I was still wearing my socks and they were wet.

"Can you do that?" She sounded confused now.

"As a private detective. I've already applied for the licence and I think I've found some premises. I even have my first client!"

She laughed. "You always did work fast, Lees. Just like your father."

I smiled at that.

"What sort of case are you working on?"

"Murder," I told her. She knew I wouldn't discuss the details.

"Ah. Bit of a busman's holiday really." She chortled. "But seriously, Lees. How can you go it alone and work on such serious cases? At least with the department, you always had someone to back you up."

And look how that had turned out.

"I can look after myself," I reminded her. Thirteen

years on the streets and a shedload of training in attack and defence magick, I knew what I was doing.

"I know that, but—"

"I might look for a partner," I told her, "but first things first, Mum. It's an expensive business getting the office up and running, and equipment and one thing and another. I don't even have a telephone line yet." I had to assume that Wizard Dodo's amenities had all been cut off. I'd have to start paying for those as soon as I could. More expense.

"That's just like your father too. Leaping into something new before you know what's on the other side."

"I tried to find other work, but no-one was biting."

"If you want a loan—"

"I really don't," I replied firmly.

"You can be so stubborn!"

"I'm big enough and old enough to find my own way in the world!"

"I don't dispute that, darling!"

"I don't need handouts."

She sniffed and I heard the chink of ice in her glass as she took a sip of her drink. "It's not a handout. It's your inheritance. I can't take it with me."

"Mum!" I hated it when she talked like this. So maudlin.

"Both your brother and your sister have had a

chunk of cash from me." That was news to me. "Your father invested it so you would all have something after we'd gone."

I knew that much. I'd never really thought about it. I suppose I'd imagined I'd tap into it one rainy day. Far into the future.

The windows rattled.

"Lees?"

It looked like my rainy day had arrived.

CHAPTER 13

I woke the following morning feeling fresher than I had in a long while. And more single-minded too. Speaking to my mother had strengthened my resolve. And as of this morning, my bank account would be five thousand pounds the richer, thanks to my father squirrelling his savings away.

I had no intention of squandering it though. Leaving the police department was a big deal. That had provided a regular salary and a decent pension. Now I was going to have to build up a successful business from scratch, which would necessarily mean a great deal of penny-pinching for a while.

I carefully packed my bag, keeping the contents to a minimum. I didn't know what today would bring. I didn't want to be gallivanting around Tumble Town with anything valuable on me. I left Dodo's notebook on the table. I wouldn't need it, and it would be safer here.

I also felt it was time to start blending in a little more with the folk on the dark side of town. Up until now, I'd opted for jeans and a tailored shirt with either my leather jacket or a light jacket. Nothing screamed affluence like clothes of that kind. From what I'd seen in Tumble Town, you either chose to wear something completely outlandish—like a hat from Hattie—or you settled for robes. I scrambled around in my wardrobe, wondering what would work, eventually selecting a plain dark dress I kept for funerals and a long black coat. It would be well worth my while investing in a proper cloak or two. I decided to ask Hattie about that. She would know someone locally who wouldn't rip me off.

But there was an additional reason for choosing these clothes.

Today I intended to dig a little deeper into what my friend Cerys liked to get up to. I was gambling on the fact that she had unfinished business in Tumble Town and, short of putting a trace on her phone calls— something I currently did not have the wherewithal to do—I was going to have to engage in a little old-fashioned police work.

Yes, today I was going to shadow Cerys and see what she was up to.

"Ministry of Witches Police Department. Good morning. How may I help?"

"Oh hi, is that Berniece?" I'd recognise her voice anywhere. Berniece had the lowest register I'd ever heard on a woman. I swear she could have sung bass. She was a lovely woman, about the same age as my mum. She'd swapped the beat for a desk job and now answered incoming phone calls when the switchboard was busy. "It's Elise Liddell here."

"Hey, Elise! How are you doing?"

"I'm fine, thanks Berniece. You?"

"Yeah, all good thanks. Long time no see. Can I help you with something?"

"I just tried DC Pritchard's direct line," I lied, "but she's not picking up."

"Isn't she?" Berniece asked. "Perhaps she hasn't come on shift yet."

"Oh, that would be it," I said. "For some reason I thought she was on earlies this week."

"Let me have a look here." She hummed to herself above the clicking of a few buttons on her keyboard. "Yep. I have the rota and it looks like she's on lates. I expect we'll see her about half one or so."

"Of course."

"Do you want me to tell her you rang?"

"No, no need. I'll call her mobile. Thanks, Berniece!"

"Any time! Take care now!"

I bided my time and, shortly before two, tucked myself behind a pillar belonging to a bank directly across the road from the Ministry of Witches. The Police Department had its own discrete staff entrance to the right of the main building, and from this perspective, I could keep an eye on people coming and going while sheltering from the drizzle. Yesterday's storm had abated, but the weather was still pretty miserable.

Any of my old team who were working the late shift would have a briefing session and a catch-up at two. The briefing usually lasted thirty minutes, depending on what was on the agenda, and then they'd be unleashed onto the unsuspecting criminal world at large.

Well, that's how I liked to think of it.

We'd all stream out of the building like worker ants, each in pursuit of a small piece of truth. Find enough of those pieces, and you could put some lowlife villain bang to rights. Nothing gave me a bigger thrill.

But now I wasn't after a supervillain or even a

common or garden crook. I was actually just mighty curious about a colleague.

There was no guarantee that she would come out of the grand old building across the road from me—one of the finest architectural gems in the country, built by Queen Victoria's husband, Albert, to house the increasingly important and ever-expanding Witches and Wizards Civil Service—she might stay at her desk and work on a case from there, but the more I thought about it, the more I was convinced that something was amiss with my friend.

I was in luck.

She stepped out of the building at around twenty to three, wearing black trousers and a beige mackintosh, a burgundy scarf tucked around her neck. I let her walk twenty yards or so before glancing all around. Satisfied that nobody was observing me, I began to tail her.

We didn't get far. She popped into Moonbucks first, a well-known chain that offered staff from the Ministry of Witches a generous discount on coffee and cake. Something I'd availed myself of many a time.

I waited patiently for her to come out, knowing she wouldn't be long. She exited the shop clutching the familiar midnight-blue cup emblazoned with a triple goddess logo and sipped at it as she wandered down Celestial Street.

I kept well back, hiding in a doorway. She could be going anywhere and, at the moment, didn't appear to be in a rush. She loitered in front of the bookshop, studying the window display, drinking her coffee. It seemed innocuous enough, but I found myself wondering why she would do that. She had been at work less than an hour, but she was taking a break already?

Or what?

I was beginning to get antsy, convinced that my cover was already blown, but then the clock in the dome above the Ministry of Witches building struck three. Cerys moved quickly, throwing her cup into the nearest dustbin and slipping across the road and down Cross Lane.

I had to break cover and follow her if I didn't want to lose her.

I waited just long enough to ensure there was no movement on her flank, and then, hugging the row of shops to my left, I began to weave in and out of shoppers until I reached Cross Lane. Now I was faced with a problem. Here, where it was widest, I could see a little way down the lane, but by the time I ventured further down the alley—because of the narrowness of the passage and the virtual enclosure above my head—visibility would be down to ten yards or so.

For one horrible moment, I thought I'd lost her

already but, as a woman with a donkey trundled past me, I caught sight of Cerys. She'd stopped to take the time to arrange her scarf around her head like a hood. The dark of the red and the black of her trousers would make it difficult to see her in the shadows. Only the beige of her coat would stand out, but even so, probably not very well.

I pulled my wand out of my pocket. She was a little further ahead of me than I'd like, but I needed to try and keep tabs on her without getting too close. I jabbed my wand in her direction. "*Bug.*"

A tiny slither of silver jumped out of the tip of my wand and flew through the air. I couldn't have aimed any better. It tagged the hem of her coat and sparkled there. Now, she could walk into pitch darkness and I'd be able to illuminate that speck of shiny silver and follow along behind.

She jerked as though she had felt something hit her. That was impossible. The silver had no weight to it at all. She turned about and I quickly tucked myself away in the nearest doorway, longing for a cloak with a hood that would have hidden the distinctive rainbow colours of my hair.

I waited, counting to sixty and then sixty again, before peering out. She'd continued on her way.

Now I had to hurry.

I tucked my wand away and reached behind my

head to grab my hair. In the absence of anything to tie it back with, I wrapped it around my fist and tied a loose knot. That would have to do. Flipping up the collar of my coat, I slipped out into the alley and hurried after Cerys.

There were so many little alleys and ginnels off the main lane, she could have disappeared along any of them, but I trusted my instinct that she would know Tumble Town as badly as I did. She wouldn't want to wander away from the well-trodden paths. She would stick to the main thoroughfares.

The shadows lengthened. By my reckoning, there should still have been two hours of daylight left, but the deeper you ventured down the lanes here, the darker the world became, until you'd be forgiven for believing night had fallen early.

I plucked my wand free as the gloom deepened. "*Illuminate*," I whispered and there, glinting like a speck of solar energy, I spied my little silver bug about sixty metres down the lane.

I must admit, Cerys was moving with surprising confidence. Perhaps it was wrong of me to assume she didn't know this area well. Perhaps my own ignorance was proving rather telling.

The lanes were busy, people moving with purpose this way and that. I had a sense that everyone knew where they were going apart from me. As they approached me, they would look away, maybe glance down at their feet or even turn their faces away, and yet I had the sense that I was being scrutinised.

I'd heard tales about Tumble Town. Haven't we all? The profusion of paranormal beings. The portals to other realms that existed somewhere without being monitored by the Ministry of Witches. I had no idea whether that was true or not, but anything was possible. It wouldn't have been unheard of for the Ministry of Witches to turn a blind eye to such a thing. Sometimes, such things would suit their purpose, and they would simply sit on their intelligence until it proved useful.

But more than anything, most 'decent' witches—or those who trod a lighter path—refused to venture to the dark side mainly because evil proliferated down here the deeper you dared to explore. An evil that was acceptable to most of the residents. Or at least accepted *by* them.

There were people here who could never have lived in the mundane world with ordinary humans. That would have been too dangerous. The mundane and the magickal needed to coexist out there in the wider world; we couldn't risk a war.

But every now and again, a witch or a wizard or a warlock broke out. At that stage, the Ministry of Witches would send teams—such as my ex-colleagues

—out on missions to find them and bring them in. If they had committed wrongdoing, they were tried and incarcerated.

But as far as possible, we as a species had to live and let live and allow the denizens of Tumble Town to create the lives they wanted as well. That was why the police seldom ventured this way, and why we left it to the Dark Squad to mop up the worst of any excesses.

I'd had so little to do with our colleagues in Tumble Town that I had no idea what kind of cases they pursued. I wouldn't even have known where to find their headquarters. Interaction between the two forces was never encouraged.

So, who was scrutinising me? Or was it my rather over-active imagination? It could have been a mugger, a warlock with an insatiable appetite for decapitating detectives, a potential serial killer, or simply kids. I didn't know, couldn't know, but I held tightly to my wand and kept my head facing forward. My eye on the prize.

Having come this far, I wasn't about to lose Cerys.

But as the lanes became narrower and even the slightest kink in the passageway removed the tiny speck of light from my eyesight, I knew that losing her was a reality. I raised my wand again. *"Vibrate,"* I muttered, and the wand twitched in my hand. The bug would emit a tiny pulse of energy from now on, and my wand would tune into it. That would allow me to keep back and out of sight. The disadvantage was that if Cerys was finely attuned and sensitive to that sort of energy, it wouldn't take her long before she realised what was happening.

I followed where the pulse led, allowing my wand to guide me. I had no idea where we were heading. Peachstone Market was as far as I'd ever made it into Tumble Town before now, but at least there it had been open to the elements and populated by relatively ordinary citizens. Here, down the labyrinthine maze that made up the eastern side of Tumble Town, it was an entirely different kettle of fish. Everything was murky here. Cobbled pavements had given way to dirt paths, barely wide enough for two people to pass. Although there was an occasional lamp burning from an iron bracket above my head, most of the light came from candles in windows. The people I passed wore dark clothes from head to foot, hats or hoods pulled low over their foreheads. I heard whispering from doorways I passed, but I kept my eyes firmly averted, unwilling to bear witness to whatever was happening down here.

And oh, the stench! The stink of a thousand tanneries. Of chemicals and sheep urine and sulphur and rotting fish. And worse. My eyes watered, and I dipped my chin beneath my buttoned-up coat, trying not to breathe too deeply.

I slithered on wet mud—and the goddess knows what else—and put my hand out to stop myself from falling on my backside, accidentally coming into contact with something loitering in the shadows. Something freezing to the touch.

"Ugh!" I jerked my hand back and sprinted forward. The ground beneath my feet changed suddenly, and I was walking on wooden boards. They sprang up as I shifted my weight. I kept going, bouncing. Ahead of me, I heard a splash and unexpectedly found myself in daylight again. I pulled up just in time. Beyond the boardwalk, with no barriers to halt my progress, the Thames was flowing past me at quite some speed. I tottered on the edge before regaining my balance.

"Whoops!" I stepped back and caught my breath. Anybody might have passed me at that stage and reached out an arm to push me in. I slunk back against the walls of the nearest building, not much more than a wooden shack made of weather-beaten planks or old ship's timbers. I rested there, allowing my eyes to adjust to the light and my new surroundings. I'd reached the very edge of Tumble Town. Across the river, ordinary humans were going about their business, living their best lives ... and here was I, deep into unfamiliar territory, surrounded by equally unknown dangers.

As I came to my senses, I realised that my wand was vibrating in my hand, not on and off as before, but with a single, continuous judder. Cerys was close by—and she wasn't moving anymore.

I glanced to my right. Warehouses and shabby sheds bordered the water leading to a quay. There were a couple of large boats moored alongside, sailors and bystanders standing around, smoking and chatting. One chap with a clipboard. No sign of Cerys. Had she climbed aboard one of those?

But why would she do that when she should have been at work? I looked to my left, peering downriver at the ramshackle fronts of more buildings. This time something caught my eye. I blinked up at a sign swinging on its sturdy iron bracket. A tavern?

I inched forwards until I could read the lettering.

The Nautical Mile!

Wizard Dodo's last memory was of eating Sunday lunch here.

This couldn't be a coincidence.

I'd reached my destination.

CHAPTER 14

I had no time to lose, but as I approached the tavern and heard music and raised voices spilling out of the open door, I realised that Cerys only had to be looking in the right direction and she would clock me as soon as I walked in.

Blast!

At that moment, a woman juggling two huge baskets of fish pushed by me. I squeezed into the wall to allow her room to pass, thankful I hadn't been on the outer edge because I would have ended up in the Thames and she wouldn't have so much as blinked.

But my scowl as I gaped after her turned into a dawning realisation. She was clad in a long skirt and shawl and a headscarf. The uniform of a fisherwoman. I darted after her.

"Excuse me!" I hissed, trying not to draw too much attention to myself. "Excuse me, madam?"

She looked back over her shoulder as she reached the turning into the lane, her eyes narrowed in suspicion. "Me?"

No doubt the use of the word 'madam' had confused her. "Yes! Hi!" I sidled up so I could speak to her quietly. "I don't suppose you would sell your shawl to me, would you?"

"You suppose right." She shifted the weight of the baskets impatiently.

"Please. I can pay." I rummaged in my bag and withdrew my purse.

She raised an eyebrow. "How much?"

How much would a second-hand shawl cost? Thirty pence in a charity shop. I decided it would be wise not to insult her though. For all I knew, the tattered rag around her neck was a family heirloom. Or had been knitted by her grandmother. "Erm, a tenner?" I drew two scrunched up five-pound notes out of the wallet part of my purse.

She peered down at the exposed contents. "Make it twenty," she said.

I puffed out my cheeks. *Extortionate!* "I'll give you twenty if you let me have the headscarf too."

"You'll be wanting my underwear next," she grumbled.

"No, no," I hurriedly told her, not even trying to hide my horror. "That's safe for now."

"Alright." She plonked the baskets onto the boards beneath our feet. They juddered. I quelled the sudden queasiness in my stomach. "Here's what I'll do for you. You can have my headscarf and shawl for twenty pounds ... if you throw in your coat."

"My coat?" To be fair I didn't wear it often, but it was pure wool and had cost me an arm and a leg.

"Seems fair to me," said a high-pitched voice in the shadows, evidently someone earwigging from a doorway in the alley.

"Pssst! Pssst!" The fisherwoman wagged her fingers at something I couldn't see. "Begone."

There was a giggle and the woman nodded in satisfaction, turning her attention back to me. "Well? What's it to be? I haven't got all day."

Neither had I. I could sense she was enjoying the negotiation far too much, and the chances were she had less to lose than I did. "Okay!" I huffed, and rapidly popped open the buttons on my coat. I patted the pockets, confirming they were empty, and stuffed my wand into my bag, glad I had elected to travel light today.

The woman watched me but didn't remove her own garments until I'd coughed up the two fivers and my last tenner. I could only hope my mother's money transfer had made it into my bank, otherwise I was a pauper from here-on-in.

She offered me her headscarf and shawl as I handed her my coat. My skin crawled at the oiliness of the material of her clothes and, as I wrapped the shawl around my shoulders, my stomach rolled at the stench of fish.

For her part, the woman seemed pleased with her end of the deal. She pulled my expensive coat over her muscular shoulders but didn't bother with the buttons. "You got yourself a bargain," she told me, and with that, hefted her baskets and continued on her way.

I swallowed the gorge that rose in my throat as I knotted the headscarf at the back of my neck and tucked my multicoloured hair beneath it, careful to scoop up all the stray strands. Satisfied that I had disguised myself to the best of my ability and, certain that my new scent—*Eau de Stinky Fish*—would at least blend in well at this end of town, I positioned my bag under my shawl and retraced my steps to The Nautical Mile. Taking a deep breath, I reminded myself of what Ezra had taught me right back at the start of my career when we had begun to work together.

It's all about confidence, he would say. *Look confident, act with confidence, breathe with confidence and all else will follow.*

You'd better be right, buddy, I intoned, and pushed through the door of the tavern.

I was surprised by how busy the place was at this time of the afternoon. Not that I knew exactly what time it was. No doubt I could have reached for my phone and found out, but that wouldn't have been a good look in a place like this. There were many people here who didn't look like they could afford an ounce of fish guts, let alone a monthly direct debit paid to some global telecommunications company. I reminded myself I was trying to vanish into the background, so I hustled to the bar with my head low, listening in to the conversations around me, paying particular attention to what people in front of me were ordering.

When it was my turn, I asked for a glass of Fire-Eye. Among the women drinking in The Nautical Mile, this appeared to be a favourite. That and Hood-winker ale. I'd have preferred not to drink at all, or at the very least order a Blue Goblin vodka, but that seemed like a rather middle-class option that would have drawn unwanted attention in a joint like this.

Fire-Eye proved to be a cheap whisky. I took a sip and winced as the liquid burned like acid as it hit my throat. I had to struggle not to splutter. I blinked away the tears that formed in my eyes, while paying the barman and turning away from the bar.

Cerys was easy to spot. The burgundy of her scarf,

a useful form of camouflage while she'd been navigating the back alleys, was a flash of colour in this tavern, chock-full of people wearing grey and blue and brown. She had a seat at a table, her back to the wall, facing me. She was keeping her head down, which played to my advantage. I realised she was probably as scared of drawing attention to herself as I was. Occasionally she looked up and sideways. I paused in place, carefully observing but without looking directly towards her. I watched her mouth move and with a start realised that she was engaged in conversation—not with anyone sitting opposite her, because the chairs were empty, but with a man sitting to her right, his body angled slightly away from her.

I say 'man', but I couldn't actually tell. Clad in long, dark brown robes, the hood pulled low over his head, I could only assume her companion was a male because of the height and build. Quite long in the body and slender.

I hesitated. I needed to get close enough to see him and overhear their conversation without making it overly obvious. My luck was in. At precisely the right moment, a couple seated directly to the left of Cerys pushed their chairs back and departed. Without thinking twice, I sidled into one of the newly vacant chairs. Now I had two options. I could face Cerys so that I could try to get a better look at the man in the robes and risk blowing my cover, or I could turn my back to them both and *listen* to their conversation.

I chose the latter.

I heard Cerys draw in a breath as I settled nearby and my stomach gave a lurch, but when she didn't otherwise react, I relaxed, guessing the gasp had been a direct response to the overwhelming fragrance of my new fishy persona.

"Next time we should meet somewhere closer to home," she said. Again, I wondered whether she was talking to me, but her companion answered, his deep grumbling voice confirming either a masculine status or a bad case of laryngitis.

"This *is* my home."

"But—"

"It's unnerving for you. I understand that," he said.

"I think that the next time we meet—"

"You'd better hope there *is* a next time. So far, you have failed spectacularly to find what I need."

"I'm telling you, it wasn't there."

The man's voice turned snide. "It must be there. He didn't take it with him, did he?"

Cerys's voice trembled. "Honestly, I turned that office upside down. I searched every nook and cranny. I flipped through the contents of every book, just about—"

They had to be talking about Wizard Dodo's office.

I toyed with my glass, straining to hear them above the hubbub of the other punters' conversations.

"*Just about* is the problem though, DC Pritchard. We think you've been careless."

We?

Cerys's voice, still low, had taken on a new pleading tone. I heard real fear there. "I swear I was as careful as I could be," she whispered. "You said not to draw the attention of my boss. And I *didn't*."

"We didn't want *anyone* to take an interest. We categorically told you we wanted the case buried."

"And it will be! You must be patient! There are processes—"

"I don't have to *must* anything!" The male, although as quiet as she, sounded enraged, on the verge of exploding.

"You have no idea how hard it is to bury a case. Especially a murder."

"Try harder."

"My colleague knows I was there."

"We can take care of him."

I swallowed. *Was that a threat?*

"Must you? No-one else has a suspicion—"

"Are you really that dense, Cerys?" the man hissed. "Someone has been sneaking around, asking questions …"

"An ex-colleague. She doesn't have any clout

anymore. Don't worry. I've been doing my best to throw her off the scent, I promise."

"But you didn't find the key. How is that your best?"

They were looking for a key? What about the one I'd found that had been stuck close to the desk's leg? Is that the one they meant?

"I packaged up everything that was in the office and had it sent to work," Cerys said. "I can go through all of those boxes again. This time with a fine tooth-comb. If it's there, I'll find it."

Her companion laughed. A low rumble. Terrible in its menace. "Never mind the boxes. You need to get back in that office and search again. Under the carpet. Beneath the floorboards. Behind the bookshelves."

"I don't have a reason to go back into his office anymore. The scene has been released back to the landlady. It will look suspicious if I start poking around again. It's better to let it be."

"I suggest you find an excuse. It doesn't matter how many of Dodo's belongings you've crated up or where you've packed them off to. Without the key, it's all meaningless. It would take a lifetime to read through everything he hoarded."

"I understand—"

"If *you* can't do it, there are others we can task with the job."

Others? What others? Did he mean other police officers? I didn't like the sound of that.

"We need the key!" he growled.

"If I knew what I was looking for—" Cerys whined.

"I've told you; nobody knows for sure. My surveillance suggests a small book."

Dodo's notebook!

A little shiver ran down my back. The notebook I had in my possession? The one I'd left at home this morning? What had I been thinking? I hadn't even locked it away!

Jeepers!

Now I was in a quandary. Either I bided my time so that I could follow the mysterious hooded figure, or I rushed home to rescue the notebook. If Cerys reached The Hat and Dashery ahead of me, she would speak to Hattie and would learn that I had rented the office above the shop. It wouldn't take her long to figure out I might have found the notebook and had been on her trail ever since.

I didn't know anything about this man in the robes, but the bleak way he laughed, his threats, the fact that he spoke of 'we' ... all of this had me worried.

This thing was bigger than I'd imagined.

I needed to put some space between Cerys and myself.

I stood, pushing my chair back a little too hard,

accidentally knocking Cerys's drink over. She yelped and scrambled around, rescuing her belongings, too busy to notice me. The robed man turned his head at the commotion. I caught a glimpse of icy blue eyes, so pale they could have been diluted seawater, and a beard with a reddish tint. He met my gaze, then nonchalantly looked away.

I shivered, anxious that even that slight glimpse would mean he would recognise me again.

I pushed past a group waiting for a table to become vacant and dodged around a trio of merry sailors blocking the door. Bursting out into the early evening air I took to my heels, not a clue how to navigate the lanes but desperate to find my way back to the relative safety of Celestial Street.

CHAPTER 15

"Where are you?" Detective Sergeant George Gilchrist sounded surprised to hear from me.

As well he might.

We'd kept in touch since working together and investigating a murder at his friend's hotel in Devon, but thinking about it, maybe that surprise stemmed from the fact that I hadn't been particularly good at returning his messages. He'd tried to be a good friend, and I had repeatedly rebuffed him. It was a measure of the man that he'd never given up on me.

The thing was, he reminded me of Ezra and how I'd lost him. I didn't want those reminders.

But now I was desperate. I had nowhere else to turn.

A couple of hours before, I had raced through the

streets of Tumble Town, unsure of the way, simply heading in as straight a line as I could manage. Twice I'd stopped people, asking them for directions to Celestial Street. I'd been lucky both times, finding people eager to point the way—rather than telling me to sling my hook, or grabbing my bag and running away. I hadn't cared who I'd barged past or knocked out of the way as I sped towards safety. Without back-up, I was a sitting duck in Tumble Town.

I was frantic by the time I'd found myself at the crossroads, the sign pointing the way home. Then, and only then, did I rid myself of my disguise, yanking the headscarf free of my head and pulling the shawl from my shoulders, chucking both into a nearby doorway.

"Oi!" I'd annoyed somebody. I didn't care. Having caught my breath I sprinted on, bursting into Celestial Street just as the clock on the top of the Ministry of Witches building marked quarter to the hour.

Nearly six o'clock.

I moved carefully now, sliding into the shadows on the darker side of the street, keeping out of the pools of illumination cast by the streetlights. Once or twice, I thought I sensed movement behind me, and I would turn and wait. Count off a minute. And then another minute. But always, there was an innocent explanation. Another pedestrian. A cat. Once a fox, its orange eyes turning to meet mine as I held my breath.

I took a detour, and then another, fretting that by now Cerys would have spoken to Hattie and know that I was renting the office. She might demand to go up there on some pretence or other. She would explain our friendship. Perhaps Hattie would refuse, but I doubted it. Cerys was a police officer. Somebody official. Hattie would feel that she had to let Cerys up there. Then my old friend would find my notes.

What a fool I was!

I'd lost my touch. I would never have made this mistake before Ezra died. I needed to pull myself together and think fast.

Would Cerys come looking for me or would she inform her 'friend'? Either way, I wasn't in a rush for a confrontation. I needed to get the notebook somewhere safe.

But where?

As I'd stood across the road, deep in the hedge, scrutinising the entrance to my block of flats, I'd half considered calling Monkton, but without knowing who was on Cerys's side, I didn't want to risk it. He was part of her team. He would trust her. Explaining what I knew would take too long. Far better for me to jump in a car and get away.

But therein lay another problem. *I didn't have a car.* I'd always driven a police vehicle—a BMW, or Beamer as we referred to them. Swish cars with great acceleration. I'd never had need of my own transport because when would I ever have a chance to drive it anywhere? On the few occasions I travelled to see family—okay, by family I mean my mum; I rarely visited my siblings—I simply borrowed a pool car.

Convinced the coast outside my block of apartments was clear, I hurried across the road and unlocked the main door, scampering up the stairs and praying I didn't bump into any of my neighbours. I paused outside my door and pressed an ear to the wood, wand poised. I couldn't hear anything inside, but that didn't mean much. An assailant could be hiding in there waiting for me. They wouldn't be holding a party to announce their intentions.

I turned the key silently in the lock, holding my breath as the tumbler clicked, then pushed it open. Creeping in, I sniffed the air, as though I'd be able to smell any disturbance. In actual fact, all I could smell was my own tangy scent.

I let out a shuddering breath and closed the door, carefully double locking and latching it. Ears straining, I tiptoed into the front room. There was the small notebook, innocuously waiting for me to come home. I reached out, my hand trembling. As my fingers made contact with the card cover, I experienced a tiny frisson of energy. Had that always been there? Had I missed it before? Or did it somehow sense that I understood its importance?

Kind of understood its importance.

I plucked it up and stuffed it down my bra, unwilling to risk slipping it into my pocket or inside a bag. Anyone desperate enough would find it, despite its rather intimate hiding place, but for now that was the best I could do.

I looked around the room. What else did I need to take? Probably only what I already had on me. A shower and a change of clothes would be good, but I absolutely could not afford to waste any time.

I couldn't think of anything else.

I checked I had my phone, double-checked that the purse I'd been carrying in my bag had my bank cards and my driving licence, and finally triple-checked that the notebook was secure.

From outside, I heard the heavy hollow thunk of the big plastic bins knocking together. It might have been nothing. Just some kids messing around. Or someone's cat trying to hide. But in my heightened state I imagined it to be something else. Without wasting another second, I unlocked my door and stepped out onto the landing. All was clear. I locked up after myself. No point in making it easier for anyone to access—

From below I heard the front door slam.

I waited, hearing footsteps coming halfway up the first flight of stairs.

Then another door opened.

"Are you looking for someone?" I heard Marian say. She sounded suspicious. Good for her. She could stall whoever it was. I slunk away from the main staircase in the opposite direction. Tucked away in the corner, behind a fire door, was a less grand flight of stairs. This led up to the roof and down to a fire exit on the ground floor, or, if you carried on down, it took you into the basement where the communal washing machines were kept.

Nobody used the fire exit as a back entrance because it had the distinct disadvantage that when you opened it, it automatically set off the fire alarm and triggered Marian's wrath. Today though, it would provide exactly the distraction I needed.

I took a mental inventory of the items on my person once more. *Phone. Money. Notebook.*

As ready as I'd ever be.

I burst through the door into the early evening as alarms began to shrill behind me.

"I'm in my car. Well, not my car. A hire car," I told George.

Thank the goddess my mother's money had cleared in the bank. Without the cash in my purse for a black cab, I'd run all the way to Waterloo Bridge—not actually that far when you know where you're going—and made it with seconds to spare before the rental place closed. The clerk hadn't been amused; I guess she was about ready to pack up and head home for the night, so I was treated to particularly sullen service. I waited with bated breath while she verified my credentials and swiped my current account card through her machine.

"Everything seems to be in order," she'd said and sniffed, then winced when she caught my stench. "There will be a cleaning fee—" she began.

"I'll pay it, don't worry." I held my hand out for the keys and she slid them across the counter, not wanting to make contact with me.

"I should walk you around the car—"

"No time, sorry." I signed the sheet she thrust at me, grabbed my bank card, receipt and the paperwork and slammed through the glass doors into the fore-court, frantically pushing the unlock button on the key fob until I spotted the flash of the silver Volvo's lights.

I drove cautiously, taking it easy as I navigated through London, but once out on the M4, I'd put my foot down, keeping a careful watch around and behind me for anything unusual.

Eventually, after two and a half nervy hours, when the M4 had joined the M5 at Bristol, I allowed myself to relax a little, reflecting on all that had happened. Perhaps I'd overreacted. Maybe I wasn't in danger at all. How much of this was in my imagination?

When the cats' eyes marking the lanes began to blur, I knew I needed to pull in for a rest. I did so at a motorway services, grabbing a sandwich and an Americano with two shots, then sitting on the front seat with the door open—to air out the car—and reaching for my phone.

I don't know why I'd called George. Just because I needed a friendly voice, perhaps. He absolutely fitted the bill.

"I'm at Sedgemoor services," I told him.

"I know it well," he said. "Are you on your way down here?"

"I—oof,"—I breathed out heavily—"it's a little complicated."

He laughed softly. "Isn't it always with you witchy types?"

He'd been involved with a witch for a while. The proprietor of Whittle Inn, Alfhild Daemonne. Hence his acceptance of who I was and what I did. I reflected that she'd been a fool to give up on him.

"I needed to get away," I told him. "Somewhere safe."

"Why?" he asked. "What's happening? Are you in danger?"

"I don't know. Perhaps. I had to get out of London. I can't say more at the moment." I glanced around the car park, examining all the cars and the people coming and going. It would be difficult to spot a threat in the dark.

"You can stay with me," he said without a moment's hesitation. *My hero.*

"Thank you." *Would that be a good idea?*

"Or ..." He paused for a moment before continuing, "maybe it would be better for you to head straight for Whittle Inn? Perhaps if you *are* in trouble, they are better placed to protect you." He sounded dubious, but also like a man who was doing his best to understand a strange situation.

"That's probably wise," I said, grateful for his quick thinking. Now that I thought about it, given the prevalence of witches and wizards at Whittle Inn at any one time, I might find someone who could help me. Silvan, Alfhild's current beau, seemed the most likely contender. Hailing originally from Tumble Town, he was a dark witch with some remarkably interesting powers.

"I'll call the inn and let them know to expect you."

"Thank you." I took a deep breath. "It makes me feel good to know that there's someone else looking out for me." Without Ezra around, who else was left on Team Elise?

"Anytime." There was a question in his voice, left unasked.

I decided to read it as concern. "Will I be able to see you?" I asked.

"Ah ... absolutely! I'm working a late shift, but I'll get off as soon as I can and meet you at the inn for a nightcap. How would that work for you?"

"Perfect," I said. "Absolutely perfect."

CHAPTER 16

"Good evening, DI Liddell." Colonel Archibald Peters—retired and deceased—Whittle Inn's receptionist, jumped up from behind the desk. I had a feeling I'd caught him napping. A short, round man, he had a bald pate and a fine curly moustache. He twitched it in my direction and waved his hand over the bell on the counter. It tinged without him making any contact with it.

A young ghost with one arm appeared. "Could you let Miss Alf know that DI Liddell has arrived, please?" Archibald asked, and the second ghost disappeared. A third appeared almost immediately in his place. I remembered this one. Florence. A Victorian house-maid or something of the sort, she'd evidently had an unfortunate accident with fire because her face was constantly sooty and her clothes puffed out ribbons of smoke. You could smell charred fabric whenever she was near.

"Good evening, DI Liddell," she chirruped. "'Tis a pleasure to see you at Whittle Inn once more. Miss Alf is just seeing to the boiler, but she's put you in The Throne Room. I can run a nice bath for you, if you like?"

She wrinkled her nose.

Touché, I thought. Florence wasn't the only one stinking up the inn tonight.

"Zephaniah will bring your bags up." She peered around me. "You do have bags, do you?"

"No," I said. "I didn't bring anything with me."

"Oh well, no matter." Nothing phased Florence. "Although I'm thinking you will need a change of clothes."

I glanced down at my black dress. It was filthy. And the smell was so strong, I could almost hear it humming.

"I'll see if Miss Alf has some clean robes anywhere." She sounded doubtful. "They might be a little roomy on you."

"I'd be grateful for anything," I said. I handed my car keys over to Archibald. "I didn't know where best to park."

"We'll take care of that," he assured me.

"Erm ... it's a little whiffy inside," I apologised.

Archibald bowed. "Don't worry about a thing. We'll take care of everything."

I swallowed the lump in my throat. They were all so kind.

"Follow me, DI Liddell," Florence said. "May I order you a drink from the bar? Or—" She studied my face, perhaps seeing the sudden emotion overwhelming me. "You look a little peaky. What about a nice mug of my own recipe hot chocolate? I always find when Miss Alf and Miss Charity are down in the dumps, it works wonders for them."

I traipsed tiredly up the stairs after Florence's floating form. "That sounds perfect," I said.

Florence was delighted. "A good choice, DI Liddell. And though I say so myself, you're right. My hot chocolate *is* perfect!"

Not simply perfect but legendary, it turned out.

As I sank into the huge bath Florence had poured for me, luxuriating in the scents of rose and bergamot with her added 'special' ingredient—a thimbleful of Dettol apparently, to help rid me of the fishy reek—she apparated in front of me and, with her gaze discreetly turned away, placed the hot chocolate on the lip of the bath near the tap end.

"That'll fix you right up, DI Liddell," she said. "I've laid out a set of robes on the bed for you for now and I will launder your other clothes, but I don't hold out much hope." She tutted sadly. "Miss Alf is finished with the boiler. She said she'll meet you in the bar unless you wish to retire for the evening?"

"No, no, I'll come down." I smiled up at Florence's sweet, scorched face. "Thank you so much. I'm feeling better already."

"At Whittle Inn, we aim to please!" she beamed, and with that, she evaporated away.

I reached for the hot chocolate and then sank back into the warm water, dabbing my tongue into the thick cream and the sprinkle of chocolate on the top. Heavenly! The chocolate itself was excellent, smooth and creamy and rich without being overly milky. I had a sneaky suspicion Florence had melted real chocolate into the drink.

By the time the bath bubbles had started to disappear—and the water had turned an odd green colour, but I'll cast a veil over that detail—and the chocolate had been drunk, I felt revitalised. I hopped out of the tub, wrapped a towel around my head and vigorously rubbed myself dry.

Alf's robes were, as Florence had suggested they might be, a little roomy, but given that robes are supposed to flow down the body, I wasn't unduly swamped by them. We were about the same height, after all.

Nervily, I confirmed my belongings were secure. My bag lay where I'd dumped it, next to the massive squidgy bed. I reached for it and located my wand, phone and notebook and plunged them deep into one of the robe's pockets. I'd hidden Dodo's notebook beneath one of the plump pillows, but now I rescued it and placed it in an inside pocket close to my heart. Florence had thoughtfully placed a pair of towelling flip flops by the door—the same kind you get in health spas—so I pushed my feet into them and made my way downstairs, following the sound of light jazz.

The bar was looking cheerful, a bright fire burning in the huge fireplace, with a variety of witches and wizards enjoying the ambience. Several of them were playing cards, and one group was gathered around a bagatelle table, howling with laughter. In a large, over-stuffed armchair, an old wizard snoozed, his beard rippling as he breathed in and out. Or I thought it was his breath. As I passed him, I realised he had a nest of mice living among his whiskers.

Nice.

Alf was perched on a barstool writing something down on a large pad, but she must have sensed me approaching because she looked up and smiled, then waved with her pen.

"DI Liddell. It's good to see you again." She sounded genuinely pleased, although given our history, maybe she was just a good actress.

"You should call me Elise," I told her. "I'm not working with the MOWPD anymore."

She nodded, her face neutral. "I'd heard. I'm sorry about that."

Maybe George had told her.

"Sorry I couldn't meet you when you arrived," she added.

"That's alright," I said. "Florence explained."

Alf wrinkled her nose. "I swear that boiler gets more and more demanding. I've had all sorts of plumbers in but none of them has managed to fix it for longer than a couple of weeks."

She squinted to the side, then flicked her eyes back at me.

I looked around, wondering what had caught her attention but couldn't see anything.

She smiled again. "I was surprised when George rang me to say you were on your way." She raised her eyebrows. I could tell she was dying to know what was going on, and why I'd raced down here from London, but was too polite to ask.

I studied the bottles behind the bar, considering what to tell her.

"Can I get you a drink?" she asked, her voice soft. She wouldn't pry if I didn't want her to.

A male voice piped up, "Make mine a pint."

I swivelled in my chair and there was George, clear blue eyes and fair hair, grinning at me.

"DS Gilchrist." It felt good to see him.

"Lovely to see you again, Elise." He leaned forward and kissed me on the cheek, then straightened up and winked at Alf.

She hopped off her stool. "Make yourselves comfortable, you pair." She waved at a free sofa. "I'll bring some drinks over."

George made a move, but I grabbed his arm and held him back. "No. Let's stay here. I need to talk this through, and I'd value Alf's input."

George nodded and slid onto the stool that Alf had vacated. She went behind the bar to pull his pint.

"I don't suppose Silvan is here, is he?" I looked around.

Alf shook her head and pulled a face. "Nope. He's away somewhere in the back of beyond and doing something dangerous and undoubtedly incredibly stupid." She studied me as she waited for George's pint to settle so she could top it up. "Did you need to talk to him?"

"Are you in touch?" I asked hopefully.

"Only when he wants to be. I haven't heard from

him for about a week." Her face fell. "Unfortunately, I can't reach him. I'm sorry."

That was a shame. I chewed on my bottom lip. Behind the bar, a bottle of Blue Goblin sparkled, reflecting the flames from the fire, gaily calling out to me. I badly wanted a glass, but if I gave in, even once, I'd never stop.

"Could I have a sparkling water, please?" I said and sighed. It was a deep, heartfelt sigh.

I caught Alf glancing to the side of me again. It was beginning to unnerve me.

"Is there some way we can help you?" George asked.

"Someone else you could speak to, perhaps?" Alf asked, unscrewing a small bottle of Magickal Falls Sparkling Essence and pouring it over ice. It hissed and effervesced in delight. Much better for me than vodka, I supposed.

"I don't know." I reached for the glass of water, noticing the slight tremble of my hand. "I've had quite a day." I laughed to offset my nerves before draining half the liquid at once.

George frowned. "Elise—?"

I stopped him, glanced over my shoulder and reached inside the robes for the notebook. I lay it gently down on the bar. Alf gazed at it from her side, George and I from ours. I slowly turned the cover, and then a few pages, so that they could see it was empty. That nothing had been written or drawn inside.

"I think a wizard was murdered for this." I spoke quietly. "I found it hidden in a secret drawer in his desk."

"But there's nothing in it," George said.

"Just because there's nothing visible on the page, it doesn't necessarily follow that it's empty," Alf told him.

"What? Like invisible ink?" George asked, reaching for the book and turning the pages himself.

"Kind of," I said.

"I suppose you've tried all the obvious spells?" Alf asked.

I nodded. "I have. But be my guest. Your magick may be better than mine."

"That would be unlikely," she said, but reached for her wand and held out her hand.

George passed the book over to her. "Imagine how quickly I could solve all my cases with a little bit of magick," he said.

"If you had murder cases that used magick, you wouldn't be the one solving them," I pointed out. That was, after all, how we had all met in the first place. "That would be my job, not yours."

Alf began a series of spells. All the ones I'd used. *Reveal. Illuminate. Show.* Bog-standard school spells. All to no avail.

Flummoxed, she handed the notebook back to me. "Do you have any idea what it contains?"

"I'm thinking maybe an index, like a written database, if that's at all possible." I shrugged. "I just have no real idea. The people who are after it referred to it as a key. You see, the wizard who was killed"—I glanced behind me and lowered my voice once more—"he was a spellcaster. That's how he made his money."

"Imagine that, a wizard casting spells." George raised his eyebrows. "Don't they all do it?"

"Yes, of course they do," I told him, amused by his complete lack of understanding of how our world worked. "Some to a greater extent than others. Almost all of my active spellmaking is tailored towards magickal police work, attack and defence. But a spellcaster is a wizard—or a witch sometimes, but less often —who has knowledge of thousands and thousands of spells. Those would include all the ones I know and all the ones Alf knows."

"I see. So he was a walking encyclopaedia of spells." George nodded.

"Exactly. But in my victim's case, he was also an archivist of spells. He actively collected grimoires and spell books and letters and magazines dating back several hundred years."

Alf perked up at this. "You think he was killed because of the notebook? Something it contained?"

"Or something that it holds a clue to?" George chipped in.

I nodded. "Yes. To both of those questions."

George picked up the notebook again, then lifted his eyes to mine. "You came tearing down here in an awful hurry."

I grimaced.

Alf breathed in sharply. "Does the murderer know you have it?"

I shrugged. "Probably."

"Did they follow you?" She widened her eyes.

"Sorry." I genuinely was. "I didn't know where else to go."

Alf made a little meeping sound. "Do you have any idea who the murderer is? Any idea what sort of trouble is liable to rock up on my doorstep?"

"Alf—" George began, but she silenced him with a raised palm.

"Don't get me wrong. I'm glad Elise has come here; I welcome it in fact. We will do all we can to help her. But forewarned is forearmed."

"That's fair enough," I said. "I think the murderer is one of my ex-colleagues. I can't swear to it yet, but she's been feeding me false information, and earlier today"—how long ago had that been? It felt like years—"I followed her to a meeting deep in Tumble Town, a tavern called The Nautical Mile, do you know it?"

Alf shook her head, her face blank. "I try not to venture too far down there."

"This ex-colleague of mine met someone there, and while I have no idea who this person is, or what he does or what his business is, I had the sense that he was part of a coven or a gang or a group." I thought back to the meeting. "He mentioned that 'we' want this, 'we' expect that." I twiddled with my glass. "The thing is, they knew someone besides the police had been looking into the case. They knew about me."

"Couldn't you have gone to your boss?" George asked. "I would have."

I exhaled. "Maybe. But the problem is ... they made it sound as though there might be more of my ex-colleagues involved. What if my ex-boss was mixed up with this?"

"Hmm. That would present a problem," George agreed.

"I just didn't know who to trust. And I *was* definitely followed back to my flat."

"Promise me you weren't followed here?" Alf asked again. I couldn't blame her for worrying.

"I don't think so. I was as careful as I could be." George and I exchanged glances. If someone really wanted to track me down, they'd find out about the hire car for starters. If DCI Monkton Wyld were involved, he would be able to trace me via the police automatic number plate recognition software. But there wouldn't be many of those sorts of cameras in East Devon, not off the main roads.

"Fair enough." Alf nodded. "I'll have a word with Finbarr about the property boundary and get Ned to do some extra security laps tonight, too." She thought for a moment. "You said he referred to a key. You made the assumption they were talking about the notebook?"

"Yes. The thing is, I did find a small brass key." I demonstrated the size. "It slotted into a hidden drawer in the victim's desk. But besides the notebook, there was nothing else in that drawer."

"No hidden drawer in the hidden drawer?" George asked. Both Alf and I shot him a look.

"No," I told him.

"So, we're going to assume the notebook is the key and that it unlocks something else," Alf said, glancing to the side of me once more.

"Is something wrong?" I asked.

"What?" She blinked.

You keep looking into space just beside my shoulder."

"Do I? Sorry! I ... erm ... yes. No, I mean." She changed the subject. "I was just thinking that I know someone who could help you with this."

"You do?" That was the first piece of good news I'd had all day.

"Yes. A wizard called Mr Kephisto. He doesn't live too far away as the crow flies. A little bit further if you're not flying."

George paled. "We won't be."

"How can this Mr Kephisto help?" I asked.

"Well, you mentioned that your wizard was a bit of an archivist. Mr Kephisto is too. He runs The Story-keeper book shop in Abbotts Cromleigh and has more books on magick than anyone else I know."

My face must have lit up. "That's a brilliant idea! Somebody like that would be more likely to know what to do."

"He might even know your murder victim. It's a bit late now, but I can take you to him in the morning, if you like?" Alf offered.

"Or I can," George jumped in.

Alf raised her eyebrows. "Aren't you working?"

"I'm on lates."

"Oh, right," she smiled.

I looked from one to the other, sensing something unspoken pass between them.

"Be my guest," she said.

"I'd like to make a start bright and early," I said. "What time do you think he would see me?"

Alf reached for George's pint glass and began to refill it. "The shop opens at nine. If you left here at about half eight you could be waiting outside when he opens."

I glanced at George. "That's an early start for you. Travelling all the way from Exeter."

Alf placed the pint in front of him and picked up his car keys. "I have a room free on the top floor if you want it," she offered. "Just ask Archibald for the key." Without waiting for a response, she moved out from behind the bar and began collecting glasses from the tables behind us, leaving us to it.

George lifted his pint. "We'll sort all this out," he said.

I reached for the remains of my sparkling water. "I'll drink to that."

"I didn't bring my pyjamas," he lamented.

"Neither did I."

He grinned. "I'll drink to that."

We chinked glasses.

CHAPTER 17

Shortly before nine the following morning I was pushing on the door of the bookshop in Abbotts Cromleigh. George had wanted to accompany me inside, but I had persuaded him to go and grab a coffee nearby and wait for me.

The Storykeeper was housed in an Elizabethan building. The front of the shop looked like the back of one of Henry VIII's old wooden ships, the stern leaning out into the street, the glass in the windows mottled with age, the timbers blackened. In many ways it looked like any independent bookshop, the window displays arranged to present a colourful array of enticing covers with a smattering of local interest books.

I'd expected the door to be locked, but as I pushed against it, it clicked open and swooshed wide. I nearly tripped over the lip of the door frame as I climbed the final step. I righted myself, closed the door behind me and navigated past a couple of free-standing book-shelves in search of a counter. I spotted one towards the rear of the shop but couldn't see anyone serving.

I knew I wouldn't have long to wait. Alf had told me she would phone him and let him know I was coming, so he would be expecting me.

"Kephisto! Kephisto!" The weird, disembodied voice came from somewhere above my head. I glanced up in surprise to meet the glittering gaze of a large black bird, sitting on a railing on a mezzanine level. A crow, I supposed, but the darn thing was enormous.

"Kephisto! Kephisto!"

I was categorically not a country girl, and animals were not my forte, so I stared at it rather distrustfully, pondering on whether to grab my wand in case it made a move to attack me.

"Kephisto—"

"Alright, Caius, alright. Steady on. I'm coming." An old man's voice.

I moved backwards so I could get a better look, and the man's head popped over the railing. He had a shock of white hair and a neat white beard, smartly dressed in a suit with a cravat, from what I could see. "I don't suppose you'd come up and meet me, would you, please?" he asked politely. "Only it will save my knees.

Living on several levels is incredibly tiresome when you have to climb up and down a hundred times a day."

"Of course!" I made my way up the stairs and found myself on the mezzanine, quite a decent-sized open space with bookshelves across the walls. It housed his local history collection, both new and used by the look of it, a spinning globe on a stand and a pair of wing-backed chairs arranged around a circular table.

"Detective Liddell, I presume?" He indicated the chairs, picking up a small book and pencil from the seat of mine so that I could sit. "I was solving some sudoku while I waited for you. Did you know that having an active brain helps to keep you young?" He didn't wait for me to answer. "I took the liberty of preparing some tea. Alfhild called to let me know you were on your way. She said you skipped breakfast." He regarded me with bright eyes, oddly reminiscent of the crow's.

"I was running late," I explained, sitting in the nearest chair. "Thank you for seeing me at such short notice."

"It's my pleasure." He smiled, pushing a plate of biscuits towards me. "Hopefully, you are here to share an intriguing little puzzle to start the day." He raised his eyebrows expectantly and tucked the sudoku book into his breast pocket.

"Did Alf say anything?" I asked.

"No, no." He took a seat and lifted the lid of the teapot to give the liquid a stir. "But I know she wouldn't send anyone to me unless she thought I could help."

I pulled my bag into my lap and reached inside it for the notebook. I moved the plate of biscuits slightly sideways and lay the book on the circular table.

Mr Kephisto studied it from a distance but didn't reach for it or immediately react. Instead, he continued with his little tea ceremony, pouring the dark gold liquid into a pretty teacup and handing it to me. "Help yourself to milk and sugar," he instructed, then relaxed back and sipped at his own.

"Thank you."

He nodded at the notebook. "How did you come by this?"

Omitting names and without getting into specifics, I relayed the details of the murder and finding the key that opened the mysterious drawer within a drawer where the notebook had been concealed. Then I told him about following my suspect deep into Tumble Town and the subsequent meeting that had alarmed me so much.

Mr Kephisto sipped his tea, his gaze steady. "Would it be amiss of me to ask who the murder victim was?"

"His name was Elryn Dodo. Wizard Dodo."

DEAD AS A DODO

"Ah, Elryn." Mr Kephisto sighed. "How sad."

"You knew him?"

"I did. We have a great deal of history. In fact"—
Mr Kephisto placed his cup and saucer on the table
—"we used to communicate regularly about his finds."

"You're a spellcaster too?" I asked.

He shook his head. "Not in the way Dodo was. I
know a little magick," he smiled, and I had a feeling he
was being self-deprecating, "but my specialism is to do
with stories in all their forms. Diaries and recordings,
letters and biographies, wills and testaments, affidavits
... that kind of thing."

"I see." *Did that mean Mr Kephisto wouldn't be
able to help me?* My heart sank.

"Now don't pull that face," he laughed. "Don't
you be writing me off yet. The thing Wizard Dodo
and I have in common was that we are both archivists.
Was, in his case. We both deal with sensitive
information."

"Can spells be sensitive?"

"There we come to the crux of the matter." He
looked pointedly at the crow. From below, I heard the
unmistakable click of the lock on the shop's front door.
"Thank you, Caius."

He reached for the teapot and refilled his cup. I
hadn't even started on my tea yet. I hurriedly did so. I
didn't want to appear rude.

235

Now he leaned forward and spoke in a low voice. "How long were you in the police?"

"Thirteen years."

"And you were regarded as good at your job?"

I nodded. There had been commendations and awards. None of those had mattered as much as getting the bad guy. Taking one more lowlife off the street. That's what had driven me.

"I'll therefore hazard a guess that you're a good person."

The straightforward way he said this made me smile. "But I am aware there are bad people out there," I politely reminded him.

"I expect you've seen some awful things in the past thirteen years."

"Of course. Some real nastiness."

"But have you ever seen any *genuine* evil?"

I thought back to the murder of my partner and shuddered. "I think so."

"There are a number of our kind out there"—he waved a hand to encompass the rest of the world, if not the universe—"who wouldn't even blink at committing the worst kinds of atrocities. There are ways and means of doing this. Having access to the right kind of magick is one way."

"The right kind of magick?"

"Or the wrong kind if you prefer."

"You're saying Wizard Dodo would have access to that?" I was beginning to see where this was going.

"Most definitely. But Elryn was not the kind of wizard to share such information willy-nilly."

"People used to write to him from all over the world asking for spells," I told him. "If someone wanted a spell for—ooh, I don't know—annihilating polar bears, and they were prepared to pay for it, are you suggesting he wouldn't have found it and sent it to them?"

"Our mundane friends are more than capable of wiping out numerous animal species without any help from bad magick," Mr Kephisto responded. "However, I *am* suggesting that the wizard I knew would have thought very carefully about supplying anything quite so catastrophic to someone about whom he had no prior knowledge. No matter what they offered to pay him."

That would have probably explained why he didn't die rich, I supposed.

"But he would have come across some extremely dark spells indeed. He would have known the whereabouts of them and their early provenance. He would have tried to find dupli-cates and close copies. I know that's the case because it's what we most regularly corresponded about."

I frowned, suddenly feeling distinctly uncomfortable. "Did he have copies of those spells in his office?"

"I should think so."

"Then that might be good news! The police boxed all of the spells up and had them shipped over to the Ministry of Witches to be stored as evidence."

"What will happen to them then?" Mr Kephisto wanted to know.

"I would imagine his property will be released back to his family."

"There was no family."

"Then it may be that we will be able to make the case that his collection remains in the Ministry of Witches' archival vault. What do you say to that?"

"It sounds like a good idea to me." Mr Kephisto nodded. "I should have some clout in that area, so leave it to me."

"But that brings us back to this." I pointed at the notebook. "Do you know what it is and why people are after it?" I picked it up and turned over a few pages. It vibrated in my hands. "Is it a key?"

"Not so much a key."

Abruptly, Mr Kephisto pushed himself to his feet. "Caius," he addressed the bird. "Keep a close eye out. Alert me to anyone showing an interest in the shop or trying to gain access." He turned to me. "Come. I'll show you what I think."

The stairs to the very top floor were disconcertingly narrow and steep. I clung onto the rail for dear life as I followed Mr Kephisto. He had mentioned his knees, but to be honest, he was sprightlier than a man half his age.

And me.

He led the way into his personal quarters—well, I assumed he lived up here, although there was no sign of a bed or anywhere to cook—and I swivelled around in astonishment. What he had up here in the attic of this three-story dwelling was a prodigious archive, rammed full of leather-bound volumes and piles and piles of magazines and journals. There were boxes too, each neatly labelled, and cardboard tubes stacked neatly on their sides containing who knows what.

"Maps and paintings," he said, as though he could read my mind. "Things of that ilk."

"Wow."

He wandered over to a bookshelf and perused the titles, head tipped to one side. "No," he said, "not these." He regarded the shelf above, running his finger along the spines. "No. Something a little older."

He bobbed away from me, six feet or so, and started to scan the shelves in front of him, crouching down to examine some tatty-edged books. "This one!" He tugged gently then used both hands to pull it free of its neighbours, reverently carrying it to his desk, where he placed it down and wafted away the dust motes that danced in the air.

"Come and take a closer look at this," he told me.

I stepped forward and peered down at the book. It had worn, flimsy covers, faded over time. The pages between had been created from cheap paper; they were starting to fray and fragment. With a nod from Mr Kephisto, I turned the cover back and began to leaf through the contents. Watercolours, like something a child might do. Blurred and indistinct. Leaves and trees maybe. Some shells. Some of the pages had writing on: badly spelled words, meaningless sentences.

"What do you see?"

I frowned. "Is it a schoolbook? A child's diary or something?"

"You'd think so, wouldn't you?" He closed the book. "This is one of the books in my collection about which Elryn and I communicated. At one stage, I took a boxful of volumes I had concerns about up to his office in London. He authenticated it."

I was confused. Why would Wizard Dodo have bothered to authenticate a child's drawing book? I'd have thrown it out.

"So, if I'm right," Mr Kephisto continued, pointing

at the notebook in my hand, "what you have there is Dodo's lifetime of work. Something so vitally important that the wrong people would kill to get their hands on it."

He reached for it and I handed it over. He gently laid the small, insignificant blank book with its crumpled pages on top of the equally insignificant child's jotter. I opened my mouth to ask about what he expected to happen but gasped instead. The notebook began to pulse and shine. Brighter and brighter, burning into my retinas and lighting up the attic with a bronze-yellow glow. I blinked and turned away until the light subsided. When I looked back, the notebook had flipped open and, where before the pages had been blank, now every millimetre of space had been covered. Tiny writings and numbers, hieroglyphics and symbols, minuscule geometric line drawings and suns, moons and stars all jostled for space.

Mr Kephisto gently lifted Dodo's notebook away from the book beneath. What I had assumed to be a child's books of drawings had transformed itself just as dramatically as the notebook had. Where previously the diagrams had been inoffensive and lacking in artistry, now they were razor sharp, as crisp and clean as the day they had been produced. And where the words had been meaningless babble, now they gave scrupulous instruction on casting the most evil of spells using toxic ingredients and vile language. I stared down at the black and red images, horrific in their graphic detail. I could feel the anger and vehemence bubbling off the pages.

I took a step backwards, bile rising in my throat.

"You were right." Mr Kephisto's tone was mild. "What you have here *is* a key, but only when placed in the wrong hands. Dodo would have thought of it as a *lock*. He used his skills to camouflage the blackest of spells, just as you see here. He would turn them into something bland and inoffensive. Something you would pass over if you found it in a junk shop or at a jumble sale."

"We have to destroy his notebook!" I said, making a grab for it. No wonder Jamendithas had told me to burn it.

Mr Kephisto, quick as a flash, blocked my hand. "We can't do that. We need it in order to locate, identify and safeguard the other spells listed within it. Without it, we'd have no head start. We'd be shouting into a void."

I pointed at the spell book in front of us. "Come on!" I protested. "No-one would have guessed what that thing concealed. The job is done."

"Unless they were specifically looking for it." Mr Kephisto picked up the notebook. It still sparkled, but the words and symbols were beginning to fade. "Even if we destroy the lock, there will still be people who have some idea of the information Dodo harboured. They will carry on searching for the material he unearthed, and what he didn't. They will stop at nothing, believe me."

That stopped me in my tracks. "Oh, crikey. That's what worries me." For a short time, I'd forgotten about the threat in London. "What if they come down here looking for the notebook?"

"We can't let them do that," Mr Kephisto said. "You'll have to go back to London. Deflect them somehow. Stop them looking for it."

I rubbed my forehead. "Ugh." I didn't know how to tell him I had no idea how to do that.

He smiled at me. "Don't worry. I may have an idea."

CHAPTER 18

"Going so soon?" George looked glum.

We were standing in the bar at Whittle Inn, waiting for Florence to fetch my clean laundry. I'd caught her on the hop by deciding to head straight back to London after finishing my meeting with Mr Kephisto. I think everybody—including me—had been expecting me to stay a little longer.

I smiled. "Why don't you come and see me when you next get a few days off?"

His face brightened. "I'd like that."

"If you time it right, you'll be able to help me move."

"I'd like that less." He smiled and flexed his muscles.

I punched his arm. "Better make it soon," I said. "If

I assume the worst happened while I was away, my landlady will want me out of my flat pretty sharpish."

Alf arrived at that moment clutching a brown paper bag and a flask. "Monsieur Emietter made you a packed lunch seeing as you didn't eat any of his breakfast. I think there's some sort of cordon bleu sandwich in there."

"And a piece of toffee and banana cake and a mini blue cheese quiche," Florence said, floating up behind her boss. "I made those myself, DI Liddell."

It wouldn't matter how many times I told Florence to call me Elise, she would still refer to me by my old title.

"And there's soup in the flask," Alf finished. I caught her glancing to the side of me once more. I shot her a questioning look and she quickly busied herself with the bag and the flask.

"I have your clothes here," Florence, oblivious, continued. "I did my best, but I think your dress has seen better days, I'm afraid."

"Did you want to change?" Alf asked. "Or you can borrow my robes for now, if you like? Until we see you again. Hopefully, that will be sooner rather than later."

I let out a jittery breath. "I hope so too."

She narrowed her eyes. "Exactly how much danger will you be in when you go back to Tumble Town?" Alf asked bluntly. There was obviously no fooling her.

I tried to keep my face neutral. I hadn't spoken to George about what Mr Kephisto had discussed. I had elected to keep everything to myself. The old wizard had provided me with a list of names who might be able to help me once I was back in Celestial Street, a few of whom would have been known to the inhabitants of Whittle Inn, I reckoned.

"I'll be fine," I reassured her.

She didn't look convinced. "I do wish Silvan had been here."

"Do you need back-up?" George asked.

I hesitated. Reinforcements would be a wonderful thing. If there was anything to miss from my old job, it was knowing that my colleagues had my back. But I couldn't ask that of him. I couldn't risk a mundane police officer following me into Tumble Town and actively investigating my case. And, given that I didn't know how many of my ex-colleagues were involved with Cerys, I didn't know who to trust. It looked like I was on my own.

"No, no," I replied, keeping my tone light.

"I could have sworn by the manner in which you flew down here only yesterday like the devil was after you that you were in a whole heap of trouble," George said, raising his eyebrows. "Didn't you get that distinct impression, Alf?"

Alf looked from me to him and back to me. "Hmm." She closed her mouth into a firm line.

George rolled his eyes. "Is there something you're not sharing?" he asked her. "I mean, what's going on here? Honour among witches or something?"

"Not at all," Alf said, "but George, could you do me a favour? Just ... step out a minute."

"Step out?" George protested. "Step out where?"

Alf widened her eyes at him. "Anywhere."

"Right. Girls' stuff, is it?" he grumbled.

"Would you like a packed lunch too, DS Gilchrist?" Florence asked, smiling brightly and gesturing towards the back passage behind the bar. "I can put one together for you if you want to choose some snacks."

"Blue cheese mini-quiche sounded nice, Florence ..." George said, following her like a hungry puppy.

"What about some cake? Or I have some freshly baked Dorset Knobs?"

"Maybe I could try both?" Their voices faded away.

I looked at Alf. She stared right back at me, her green eyes curious. "How much danger are you in?"

"Nothing I can't handle. Hopefully." I shrugged. "You're surely not thinking of coming with me?"

"I would if I could, but Charity is on a break with her man, Grandmama has disappeared, and ..." she faltered, "… I can't imagine I'm the help you need in any case."

"It was good of you to consider it," I told her. I pulled my purse from my bag. "How much do I owe you for my stay here?"

"Pfft!" Alf waved me away. "You're welcome here anytime—"

"But—"

"I did it as a favour to George. And besides, we owe you."

She meant for what had happened when Ezra and I were investigating a murder here. I shook my head. "You don't."

Alf took a breath. "Elise?"

I waited. She had something to say. I expected an apology. I didn't expect her next question.

"You *can* see ghosts, can't you?" She tipped her head to study my reaction.

"Some." I thought back to my encounter with Wizard Dodo. I hadn't been able to see him, only hear him. "When they want to be seen."

"And when *you* want to see them," Alf said, and her voice was gentle now.

What was she getting at? Suddenly, I didn't want to know. "Don't," I said, taking a step away from her.

"Only it strikes me that if you need back-up, and if

you want a partner for your detective agency, he's been with you all this time."

My eyes filled with tears. "Stop," I said, my voice little more than a whisper.

"You only have to call him. He's following you around, waiting for your sign."

I rubbed my eyes. "I really need to get going. I can't deal with this now."

"Alright. He'll be there when you're ready."

She was being kind. On impulse, I reached for her and hugged her.

"We'll be here if you need us," she said. "All of us. All you have to do is call."

"Thank you."

We broke apart as George's voice drifted down the passageway, coming closer. "You didn't need to give me two pieces, Florence."

"Oh, I expect you'll polish them off in no time, DS Gilchrist. Get away with you."

CHAPTER 19

"Elise?" Hattie peered through the tiniest of gaps from behind the side door. The Hat and Dashery had been boarded up. Here, on the outside, I could still see slithers of glass among the cobbles where it hadn't been properly cleared up.

"What happened?" I asked, my heart sinking. I'd brought this on her. I knew that without a shadow of a doubt.

"The shop was attacked last night." She kept her voice low, evidently fearful of being heard. The one eye I could see through the slit scanned the lane, perhaps searching for undesirables.

"Did you call the police?"

"No," she said, and there was something I couldn't identify in her voice. "I didn't."

She closed the door. I stared at it in surprise. I'd

tried to gain entry to the building with the key she had given me, but my progress had been barred by the chain across it. My rattling had alerted her, and she'd come downstairs. Unwilling to bully Hattie, especially given that she must have been traumatised by events, I resisted the urge to bang on the door and demand she let me in, no matter how panicked I felt.

I didn't have to.

Hattie slid the chain back of her own accord, pulled the door open a little wider than before, reached out to grab my arm and hauled me inside. She slammed the door behind us and, locking it, gestured for me to go up. I did so, waiting on the first-floor landing until she joined me, then followed her inside her apartment where once again she locked the doors.

When she turned to me, I saw her properly for the first time. She had a black eye and a cut across the top of her nose.

"Hattie!" I reached for her in a panic. "What happened here?"

"Don't fuss, my lovely," she told me, "it looks a lot worse than it is."

"But still—"

"Hush." She gestured towards the living room and we went in and took a seat. Or rather, I perched, as tense as a coiled spring.

"It was my understanding the police had finished upstairs," she started.

I nodded. "They had."

"After I said I'd let the room to you, I locked it all up. But, late yesterday afternoon, that young woman police detective person came round here wanting to go upstairs. I wasn't keen. No need for people to be coming and going anymore after all, is there?"

"No," I agreed.

"She said she had forgotten something, which I found strange, but I did let her in and then went back to what I was doing in the shop. After a few minutes I thought to myself she'd looked a bit harassed. Kind of out of breath and wild-eyed and red in the face ... and ..." I could see Hattie casting her mind back, remembering the details. I loved witnesses with good recall, and it seemed Hattie was the best, "... even scared. So I figured something wasn't quite right. I locked up the shop and went up there, and she was going through your things!"

"The notes I'd left on the desk." I'd known that would be the first thing she'd find.

"So I corrected her, sharpish! I said, 'those are Elise's things, dearie. They've nothing to do with poor old Wizard Dodo's death.'"

"How did she take that?"

Hattie smirked. "She wasn't best pleased, if I'm

honest. Started ranting about how I was interfering in police business. Well, I put her straight, I can assure you." Hattie folded her arms across her impressive chest and glared at the memory.

"Go on."

"I told her that the handsome head detective person—"

"DCI Wyld?"

"Yes, him. I told her that he'd released the room back to me and told me I could do what I liked with it. I said that if she wanted to gain access to it, she would have to get a warrant."

I stared at Hattie in surprise.

"Do you think I've been watching too many detective shows?" she asked.

"Probably," I said.

"So she hit me."

I couldn't have been more astonished. "Cerys hit you? DC Pritchard?"

"Punched me right between the eyes. Nearly broke my blooming nose!" She dabbed tenderly at the cut.

"Ouch," I sympathised.

"Ouch indeed." Hattie looked momentarily annoyed but then broke into a grin. "So I punched her right back."

I couldn't help it. I laughed. "You didn't!"

"Oh yes I did! You don't mess with us Tumble

Town folks. I punched her hard enough to put her on her back." Hattie beamed with pride.

"So what did she do then?"

"She made a run for it. Fell down the top flight of stairs. Managed the last one alright. I chased her down them, though. I was all for giving her another walloping."

What a feisty little woman Hattie was. I clapped my hands in delight.

Hattie shrugged. "Course, she came back after midnight and put a couple of bricks through the windows downstairs."

"It was definitely her?" I asked.

"Well, no, I suppose not. But who else would it have been?"

The people she's in league with. Whoever they are.

"Oh, I'm sorry about the damage and the fuss, Hattie. I feel like I've brought it on you."

"Don't be daft!"

"If you don't want to let the office out to me anymore, I'll completely understand." I stared at her with what I hoped was my most pathetic and woeful expression.

She batted at the air as though to wave my concerns away. "We shook hands on it, didn't we? Hattie Dashery doesn't renege on a deal."

I climbed the stairs to the office with some trepidation, but Hattie must have interrupted Cerys before she could do any real damage. All of my notes were there, scattered around the desk and the floor. I sorted through them, trying to calculate how much Cerys had been able to read before Hattie disturbed her.

Long enough, I decided.

She would know I had suspicions about the murder weapon. The newspaper clipping that Wootton had given me was among the files. She knew I knew that she had been in the area on the night of Dodo's murder. She knew that Snitch had heard police radios, implicating more than one police officer.

Had the mysterious robed figure at The Nautical Mile told her I'd overheard their conversation?

Unfortunately, she would also understand that most of the evidence I had was circumstantial and wouldn't stand up in court. A jury would never believe Snitch—currently languishing on remand for the same murder—over the sworn oath of a respected police officer.

And now, although I understood what the motive had been—I tapped the notebook I'd hidden in the inside pocket of my robes—I didn't have a clue who Cerys was working for. Neither had I figured out, besides DC Kevin Makepeace, whether any other police officers might be involved.

Those were the things I needed to find out.

I straightened up my desk. Not a lot of point in locking anything away; the deed had been done.

I pulled out the list Mr Kephisto had collated for me. People I could approach. A handful of names of witches and wizards he trusted implicitly. Chief among those was Wizard Shadowmender, whom I'd met previously. Perhaps he would be able to help me.

I locked up the office and descended to the next level to say goodbye to Hattie. "Call me if you have any more problems with bullies," I told her. She promised she would, following me down to the ground floor to double-lock the front door after me.

Only once I'd heard the chain slide across did I walk away. I hurried along Tudor Lane, passing The Pig and Pepper on my right. I popped my head inside, seeking Wootton, but perhaps he had a shift off. I couldn't immediately see him, and I didn't have time to wait.

As I backed out of the door, someone clamped a hand on my right shoulder. Without thinking, I ducked and swivelled hard to my right, taking my assailant by surprise. As I stood, I lifted my elbow and jabbed sharply at his face.

"Ooof!"

The man clasped his nose and took a few involuntary steps backwards, colliding with the heavy front door and banging the back of his head, then sliding to a sitting position on the cold, tiled floor.

I planted my balance firmly through my left side, prepared to give him a swift kick to the side of his face with my right foot, but he raised his hands, blood streaming from his nose. "I surrender, Liddell! Enough!"

"*Monkton?*"

"That's DCI Wyld to you!" he grumbled.

"Whoa!" Wootton appeared from nowhere. "That was awesome!"

I glared at the young bartender. "You could be useful and get some ice."

"I'm just saying, those are admirable skills, Grandma. We could use you as a bouncer in here over the weekends."

"Ice!"

Wootton grinned and strolled behind the bar.

I turned back to Monkton. "I'm so sorry! You caught me by surprise! I thought you were attacking *me.*"

He brushed my hands away as I tried to help him stand. "And I thought *we* were on the same side. The goddess help those who get on the wrong side of you!"

Against his protestations, I led him to the bar and

helped him sit on a stool. Wootton handed over a clean bar cloth—at least I hope it was clean—and I tipped ice onto it and twisted it to make a cold compress. Handing it to Monkton, I said, "Here. Put this on your nose."

"I'll have a whisky too," Monkton mumbled from behind the compress. "For the shock."

I nodded at Wootton.

"You can pay, can you?" Wootton wanted to know.

Cheeky beggar. "Yes!"

"Make it a double," Monkton said and, rolling my eyes, I agreed.

"Anything for you, Gr—" Wootton started. I scowled at him. If he called me Grandma just once more, I was going to level him as well. He must have recognised my fury because he stopped himself, just in time. "Would you care for a drink, Ms Liddell?"

"No, thanks. I need to get going."

"Going?" Monkton took the ice away from his nose. I winced. It had started to swell up; I hoped I hadn't broken it. "Where are you going?"

"Things to do, people to see. You know how it is." I patted his arm. "Wootton will look after you."

"Will I?" Wootton handed over Monkton's double whisky. "I'm no nurse."

"But you are a caring person," I chided him.

I turned back to Monkton. "What were *you* doing here, anyway?"

"I fancied a drink."

The lie was so ridiculous, I guffawed. "In The Pig and Pepper?"

"Do you mind?" Wootton said, affecting a look of deep hurt. *Entirely* affected, of course. This place was the pits, and he knew it too.

I handed over a tenner to pay for Monkton's drink and accepted the change Wootton grudgingly offered.

"I'd love to stay and chat," I told them both, "but as I said, I need to get going."

Monkton dabbed at his face. "I'd say mind how you go, but I think you've got that covered. The bad guys must run and hide when you're in the vicinity."

"Ho ho ho." I waved my goodbyes.

As I exited The Pig and Pepper, I realised it had started to spot with rain while I'd been otherwise engaged inside. I pulled the hood of Alf's robe over my head, pondering on what Monkton had been planning to get up to all the way out here in Tumble Town. I knew he liked a drink, but on his own in Tudor Lane? That didn't seem likely to me.

Had he been heading towards The Hat and Dashery? Searching for me? Or had he been looking to make trouble for Hattie? I glanced left up the lane, towards the boarded windows of Hattie's shop. I could see the muted glow of light from the window in her apartment.

Or ... had Monkton been planning on a secret rendezvous?

Who?

No sooner had that thought materialised, than I heard soft footsteps ahead. A figure darted into the shadows on the opposite side of the lane.

In Tumble Town everyone has something to hide, so there was nothing unusual about this person's actions. And yet ... something in the manner in which they'd moved had caught my attention. And although I'd only glanced at them for a fraction of a second, the shape, the height ...

It had to be Cerys.

I crossed the lane in a couple of steps and flattened myself against the building there, then quietly stole towards the last place I'd seen her. Watching out for her, I inched towards a doorway, reaching inside my robes for my wand.

I peered around the corner of the wall, ready to either duck or attack. The doorway was empty.

A little further up ahead, something heavy clanged. An iron door. Like the ones in the factory across from The Hat and Dashery.

But that was abandoned. Empty. Locked up.

Wasn't it?

I glanced behind me. No-one there. Light spilled from The Pig and Pepper and I could hear the heavy beat of a metal track. Had Monkton intended to meet Cerys? It was a bit of a coincidence them both being here. I edged forwards again, heading towards the factory, ears and eyes straining.

I approached warily, treading quietly, controlling my breathing. The blood raced around my veins. Nerves. Excitement. The thrill of the chase.

I tipped my head back to stare up at the antiquated three-storey building. Older even than The Hat and Dashery, the top of this once impressive structure leaned forward as though to kiss Wizard Dodo's office. It was still and quiet and shrouded in darkness.

But then I heard the unmistakable sound of breaking glass from within.

Whoever was in there, regardless of whether it was Cerys or not, they were trespassing.

I grabbed the handle of the iron door and pulled. It was stiff and heavy but swung out quietly enough. Inside, the room was in complete darkness. Once I closed the door behind me, it would be pitch black. If I lit the tip of my wand, I would make myself a target.

I looked around for something to jam the door open with. Luck was with me. To the side was an old and rusted fire extinguisher. I hefted it, expecting it to be weighty. Unfortunately, someone—kids probably—had let it off at some time in the past. Nonetheless, it was solid. I used it to wedge the door slightly ajar, then quickly moved into the shadows.

I crouched down, regulating my breathing, allowing my blood to settle and my eyes to adjust to the darkness. Once I could see, I peered around. Most of this floor appeared to be open plan. A few doors at the opposite side to where I was hiding suggested small rooms, perhaps bathrooms. Beside me was a corner office or reception, the glass long since broken.

An iron staircase led to the first floor. With no apparent sign of life down here, it appeared I would need to make my way up.

Carefully I stood, watching where I trod, cautiously approaching the stairs. I sensed, rather than saw, movement up above, as though the air had been disturbed. I put one foot on the first stair and began to climb. Slowly, one foot at a time, pausing between each step to listen and look, I ascended. When my head was at floor level, I waited a moment, training my eyes. There was hardly any light up here. The windows were boarded up. What little light I had let in by leaving the door ajar on the ground floor didn't reach this far.

Something fluttered directly above my head. My

body jerked reactively away. Although startled, I didn't think twice. I shot my wand, aiming by instinct, while simultaneously pitching forwards. I rolled, glass crunching beneath me. The 'something' squawked. It hit the floor next to my head with a soft thump.

A pigeon. *Oops*.

I exhaled. *Soz*.

Pushing myself up to a sitting position, I waited. I'd made enough noise to alert anyone to my presence.

There's probably not much point in being subtle anymore.

"Cerys?" I called and illuminated the tip of my wand, shining it into the recesses of the building. This was another open-plan floor, but with a variety of old machines scattered about, some free-standing, some on tables. Junk was strewn all over the place: bits of twisted metal, rotten newspapers, old wooden crates and pallets, broken glass from the windows, a mattress and a few odd shoes.

I heard shuffling in the far corner, followed by the clunking of boots on iron rungs. Cerys was making her way up to the top floor. I pushed myself to my feet, wincing as a piece of glass embedded itself in the palm of my hand. From downstairs came a clang. The front door hitting the fire extinguisher.

I had company.

And they would have already seen the light thrown

off by my wand.

Frowning into the stairwell, I ground my teeth together. That's all I needed, to be the filling in an Elise Liddell death sandwich.

Seeking to fade further into the already impenetrable shadows, I crept backwards, away from the stairs. It was impossible to move quietly: my boots crushed the glass beneath my feet. Every step I took gave away my position.

I stretched my neck, peering towards the stairs, hoping to see who the newcomer was. The floorboards above my head creaked, sending down a shower of ceiling plaster, reminding me of the danger from above. The footsteps below paused, but only momentarily, then headed for the stairs, their pace quickening.

I continued to back gently away, toe to heel, toe to heel, trying to put some distance between us, desperately searching for something among the detritus large enough to hide behind.

"Elise? Did you come in here?" A familiar voice at the foot of the stairs. Slightly more snuffly than normal. "Elise?"

Monkton!

I hesitated. *Why had he followed me?*

I kept moving away, trying to creep. A loud thump above my head startled me and I mis-stepped, sending a tin or something similar skittering noisily away.

Drat!

"Elise?" He was on the stairs now.

I readied my wand, keeping my breathing under control. Waiting for the right moment.

Waiting.

Waiting.

And there he was, at the top of the stairs, moving with caution, radiant in the light from my wand.

"Stay where you are," I warned him.

He wasn't listening. "What are you up to?" He moved away from the stairs, coming towards me.

"Stay where you are, Monkton!"

Momentarily distracted by him, I didn't see the shape that flew up from the floor. Before I had a chance to react, it screamed in my face. The high-pitched wail, emitted at a frequency that would probably send the dogs of Tumble Town berserk for a radius of approximately ten miles, threatened to burst my eardrums. I shrieked and tried to strike out. The shape had already darted away—a robed figure, ridiculously thin. So thin it seemed to lack proper substance.

I raised my wand to take aim at it, but it had flown at Monkton and as he, entirely unprepared, fumbled for his wand, it knocked him backwards, sending him crashing to the floor. Job done, it spun to face me.

Confused, I faltered. If this thing was attacking my old boss, did that mean Monkton wasn't on their side?

Or maybe I was fighting two different enemies here. Should I—

A terrific crash above my head caused an avalanche of plaster to fall, spattering me with large lumps. I threw myself sideways, my wand flying from my grasp. Above me, a woman screamed—it had to be Cerys—as part of the ceiling caved in where I'd just been standing.

I scrabbled among the dust and the broken glass for my wand, my gaze swivelling between the hole in the roof, the dark-robed figure and Monkton. Poor Monkton appeared to be out for the count, but at least that was one less thing for me to worry about. His assailant flew at me, a good eight inches off the floor, covering the distance between us quickly.

I spotted my wand, painfully out of reach, so I held up my left hand. "*Murus!*" I ordered, and the creature, whatever it was, jerked to a sudden stop. It was a temporary fix. The robed figure curled a twisted skeletal hand and tapped at my makeshift barrier. The energy I'd harnessed exploded in a shower of sparks. I'd won myself just the right amount of time to grab my wand. I levelled it at the creature. "*Obstupefacio daemonium!*" I cried, preparing myself for the thing to come straight at me, but the robes—abruptly emptied of all life—collapsed to the floor, emitting a supernatural hiss and a cloud of sour-smelling vapour. I rolled to my feet and quickly stamped on the steaming bundle. Nothing there.

Monkton sat up, blinking at me. "What's going on, Elise?"

A second bloodcurdling shriek above our heads had us both glancing upwards. "Stay there," I told him and ran for the stairs in the corner. I say stairs, but to be honest, they were little more than an iron ladder strategically placed at an incline. I didn't hesitate. I stamped up it, ignoring its odd sponginess, and burst onto the top floor.

Up here, the windows hadn't been boarded up. Given the proximity to the building across the way—Dodo's office—only a limited amount of moonlight and light from the street below filtered in. There were small holes in the roof, which allowed the rain to seep in. Everything felt damp and cold and precarious. Cerys lay flat on her back next to the hole in the floor, her eyes open, staring at the beamed ceiling above. I feared, at first, she might be dead but, sensing me, she lifted her right hand.

I carefully walked towards her, scanning the shadows under the eaves. The floor bounced beneath my feet and my pulse raced. What if the floor wouldn't hold my weight? What if—

But then I was beside her. I crouched next to her and felt for the pulse in her neck. It was beating strongly. She was going to be fine. "Can you speak?" I asked her. "What happened here?"

She mouthed something in response, but I couldn't hear what it was. I leaned over. "Say again?"

A fluttering sound. A light breeze. Iron fingers clamped around my neck. Something yanked me away from Cerys and threw me across her. I tumbled and landed close to the edge of the hole. I shrieked, my arm and shoulder grasping at thin air, my torso beginning to slide.

Then the thing had me again. It turned me about so my head dangled into the gap, my hair flowing free. If it let go of me, I was a goner. Gravity would pull me through the hole and I'd crash onto the machines below. It wouldn't be pretty. With some difficulty, I lifted my head and stared up into ... empty robes. Where the face should have been, there was a black void.

"Please," I begged.

It tightened its grip on my shoulder. I was putty in its bony hands.

"The key," it said, in a voice like tearing paper. The words were taken up by others I couldn't see.

"The key!" The words echoed around the room. "The key!"

How many of them were there?

I swallowed with difficulty and lifted my right

hand. It held my wand and the creature hissed angrily. For just a second, I thought I saw the outline of a face. The sharp lines of a skeletal face. Pale eyes. Transparent.

I dropped my wand before it decided to drop me. "It ... it's in my pocket," I gasped and pointed at my chest.

"Give it to me!"

"Give us the key!" The cry was taken up by those unseen others.

"The key!"

Hands trembling, I reached inside my robes and located the notebook I'd stored in the inside pocket next to my heart. All fingers and thumbs, I had trouble extracting it. The card outer caught on the inside lining. My breath wheezed in and out of my throat. If I handed the notebook over, I was convinced this being still intended to let me fall.

I was going to die.

And yet what other option did I have?

I tugged the notebook free.

The iron staircase clanged, and I turned my head. Monkton picked that moment to clamber up the stairs. He took one look at the scene and froze; if he aimed at the robed creature, I would fall through the hole.

Monkton's eyes met mine in desperation. He had no idea what was happening. I hadn't shared my suspicions about Cerys, and that had been an error on my part. But hindsight is all very well when you're just about to impale yourself on some fierce-looking antique industrial cotton-picking machine. He had a choice to make.

He raised his hands in surrender and the creature snatched the notebook from my hand. It tossed its head back and emitted another of its deathly shrieks, then leapt for the nearest window, crashing through it and tumbling away. As other shadows darted from beneath the eaves, cackling, howling and screaming, I began to slide. My right hand tried to find something to grab onto, but I was slipping inexorably downwards.

Fortunately, Monkton hadn't been distracted by all the activity. *"Levitate!"* he yelled above the din, and a cushion of warm air pushed me up. Then he was there, grabbing hold of me and dragging me away from the hole in the floor.

As soon as my backside touched solid ground, I fought the urge to retch and shot straight to my feet. I threw myself at the window and leaned out, straining to see. Below us, Tudor Lane was quiet and still, the damp cobbles shining in the streetlights. From somewhere, I heard the sound of breaking glass and the forlorn cry of a cat.

The robed figures had melted away into the darkness.

CHAPTER 20

I've never had an out-of-body experience before, but I think in the few hours immediately after creeping into that wretched warehouse, I probably experienced one.

Monkton, fortunately only a little battered and bruised, called out his colleagues and an ambulance. By the time the paramedics arrived—wheeling a gurney up the street because there was no way a vehicle would have made it along Tudor Lane without getting permanently wedged—Cerys was catatonic, unable to do anything except blink. They took her away, and I watched them manoeuvring her over the cobbles, unable to feel anything like sympathy for her.

But neither did I feel angry.

They had bandaged the gash in my palm and told me it needed stitches, but besides that and some bumps and bruises and broken fingernails, I'd come through the encounter relatively unscathed.

"What were you pair doing here?" Monkton asked, seemingly bewildered by the turn of events.

"What were *you* doing here?" I retorted. I still hadn't shaken my suspicions.

He dabbed tenderly at his nose. "I told you. I just came out for a drink."

It suddenly occurred to me that he might have been hoping he'd find me in The Pig and Pepper. Maybe he was as innocent as he claimed.

I drew in a shaky breath, counted to five, then let it go. "I could really go a vodka," I told him.

We walked together in silence away from the factory and, by silent mutual consent, perched on stools at the bar.

"Yowza," said Wootton, scanning our faces and no doubt taking in the dusty state of our clothes. "You've only been gone forty minutes." The stink of mildew clung to my robes, but I was so tired, I hardly cared. He poured Monkton a shot of whisky without asking before crooking an eyebrow at me. I stared at the bottle of Blue Goblin, sparkling on the optic behind the bar. Beautiful vodka …

"Coffee," I said.

"Please," Wootton sniped.

I stared at him. He folded his arms and stared right back at me.

"You have no manners," he said.

"You have no customer service skills," I retorted.

"People like *you* are *why* I have no customer service skills."

We glared at each other.

Then he smirked. And broke out into a smile. It lit his whole face up, like the sun coming out on a stormy day.

I laughed.

"Do you want a job?" I asked. "I could do with someone like you in my office."

Wootton looked pleased but suspicious at the same time. "Doing what? Under-detective?"

"There is no such thing," I told him. "It would be a"—I had to think on my feet—"secretary-receptionist-computer-support-researcher type role."

"Ooh. Varied. And you can pay me?"

"As long as you can help me bring in more money than I'm paying out, yes."

"It's a deal." He handed me my coffee. "See you tomorrow at nine."

I nodded at him and took the mug. "Make it ten," I said. "I need a lie-in." *And I haven't been home and seen the state of the flat yet,* I reminded myself.

"No problemo!" Wootton wiped the bar clean of smears. "Grandma," he added.

"Are you going to tell me what's been going on?" Monkton and I had moved into a booth for extra privacy. He was clutching his head. I reckoned he had a headache that he wasn't owning up to. "What were those ... things?"

I held my coffee with one hand, staring down at the blood seeping through the bandage on the other. *Oh yeah, I need stitches.*

"I don't know what or who they were. I was hoping you would."

"What did they want? They weren't messing around."

"It's a long story," I told him.

"The night is still young, and your new employee has plenty of whisky behind the bar."

"Your head won't thank you if you overdo the whisky."

"Two headaches for the price of one. Bargain." He pointed at my coffee. "I'm impressed with your resolve."

"This stuff won't help me sleep though," I sighed. Although to be fair, my mind was full of the day's events. Had it really been less than twelve hours since I'd left Mr Kephisto in Devon?

"Spill the beans, Elise," Monkton said. "The sooner you get to it, the less drunk I'll be."

"Alright." I began to recount the whole story, including what he already knew about how Snitch had led me to Wizard Dodo's office, right through to the moment he'd followed me into the old factory.

"And the rest you know," I finished.

"DC Makepeace?" Wootton crinkled his brow. "He's taken a leave of absence."

"Unexpected?" I asked.

Monkton nodded. "I might have to look into that." He raised an arm and gestured for Wootton, loitering at the bar, to refill his glass. "Do you seriously think Cerys killed Dodo?"

"I do, but I can't prove it, unfortunately. It's not crystal clear to me that she went up to his office on Sunday night with the *intention* of killing him. Maybe she'd been sent there to intimidate him. I'm fairly certain she killed him with his own letter opener. It's never been found, but we know it was there in the days before his death because *The Celestine Times* ran a feature on him, and the photo clearly showed the letter opener on his desk."

Wootton had returned with a fresh glass for Monkton.

"That was a useful bit of investigation from my new researcher," I acknowledged. "It suggests she didn't *intend* to kill him when she entered his office; she was only supposed to secure the key."

Monkton frowned. "It's the strangest story—"

"But not a story at all."

"You don't seem overly upset about losing the key."

"Of course I am!" I protested. "I'm completely gutted! But what could I do? It was me or the key!"

He frowned.

I planted my head face down on the desk, hiding my face. "I'm shattered," I mumbled. "I'd like to get the key back, but I don't know who those robed figures were. Where would I start?"

He squeezed my shoulder. "Why don't you go home and get some sleep? I'll put some feelers out in the morning. See what I can find out about them."

"And Cerys?" I sat up and brushed my hair away from my face.

Monkton grimaced. "What do we have to hold her on?"

I tutted. Sometimes the justice system could be so unfair.

"I can put her on leave for a while. That will give us time to investigate further."

"And Snitch?" I waggled a finger at Monkton. It

seemed a lifetime ago since I'd asserted Bartholomew Rich's innocence.

Monkton conceded defeat. "I'll get him released."

"Tonight?"

"Give me a break, Elise. As soon as I get into work in the morning."

"Alright." I drained the last of my coffee. "Well, there is one positive to take away from all this, at least."

"What's that?" Monkton was beginning to look glassy eyed.

"At least you have all of Wizard Dodo's books and letters and personal belongings in storage at the Ministry of Witches."

"What are you talking about?"

"I told you," I reminded him. "Cerys informed me that everything from the office had been taken into evidence. If Dodo's life's work is locked up in the police department, there's no chance it will fall into the wrong hands. It means that regardless of the fact that the robed figures—whoever they were—got hold of the key from me, they won't be able to do any lasting damage."

Monkton paled and leaned forwards, shaking his head ever so slightly. "I have *some* of Dodo's belongings bagged as evidence, but not the entire contents of his office—"

"But I saw everything bagged and boxed up," I

insisted. "Cerys was overseeing that with Makepeace, and she told me—"

"It didn't come to us. Cerys must have had it moved elsewhere."

"Oh, my." I sank my head into my hands, weary beyond belief. "That's a disaster."

"I'll get onto it tomorrow, I promise. Hopefully, DC Pritchard will be well enough to talk to me. She has some explaining to do."

"Good luck with that." I slid out of the booth, completely horrified by the news that all of Dodo's archive was missing. "I'd better go."

"Will you be alright getting home?" Monkton asked. "I'm happy to walk you."

I nodded. "I'll be fine. You've done enough for one day. Thanks for saving my life."

"It was my pleasure." He tipped his glass at me.

I waved goodbye to Wootton and traipsed outside. As the door to The Pig and Pepper closed behind me, I straightened up and stared down the lane.

Was it my imagination, or did the shadows shift and quiver just out of my immediate eyeline?

I would find out who those robed figures were, I swore, and bring them to justice.

But not tonight.

I retraced my steps to the Hat and Dashery and, using a neat little spell I'd learned at police college, gently and quietly slid the chain back and unlocked the door. A kind of magickal equivalent to picking a lock, really. Once inside, I locked up behind myself.

I snuck upstairs to the office and let myself in. I had no intention of going home in the dark. The devil alone knew what kind of mess would be waiting for me there and how many of my belongings I'd be able to salvage. I hoped Hattie wouldn't mind me camping out in the office until I could find somewhere else to live.

I settled myself down on Dodo's chair. The very one in which he'd been murdered. Perhaps it should have seemed a little morbid, but I recognised it as a small tribute to him.

I reached for my phone, scrolled through the list of contacts and found the one I wanted. I hit dial. It was late, but I'd promised I'd call.

"Good evening, Elise." Mr Kephisto's gentle voice.

"It's done."

"Good. I hope you weren't hurt."

"Nothing that a few days won't heal," I said, turning my left hand over to stare at the bloom of blood on the bandage. I really needed to get it sorted.

He giggled softly. "Let's hope they like sudoku."

That had been his plan. He had enchanted his puzzle book to make it a carbon copy of Dodo's note-book in every way, even down to the gold shimmer and the teeny pulse of energy. He'd added layers of locks and puzzles to the notebook that would need to be deciphered before anybody could discover exactly what a dud they'd stolen from me.

It would give me time to investigate further. Dodo would not go unavenged. Not on my watch.

"The bad news is that Dodo's archive was not sent to the Ministry of Witches."

Mr Kephisto made a small noise at his end. "That is a problem. Leave it with me."

"And the other thing?" I asked. I meant the other notebook. The real one.

"It's safe."

I breathed out in relief, feeling some of the tension ebb away. "Excellent. Goodnight."

"Goodnight." He hung up.

I placed my phone on the desk and sank into the chair, looking out at the dark factory windows opposite.

I could relax.

At least for a while.

"Could you look this way please, Elise?" The photographer from *The Celestine Times* was trying to take a photo for an article the newspaper was running on the launch of my detective agency. We were standing in front of the newly replaced glass windows of Hattie's shop. She had created a wonderful display of colourful top hats especially for the occasion and given me one I could wear for the photos.

I'd worn it to please her, and because it was a generous gift, even though I'd spent a small fortune at the hairdresser's having new rainbow streaks threaded through my hair.

I suppose a little bit of free publicity never hurt anyone. Hattie was certainly getting plenty of that. We'd drawn quite a crowd. Snitch, Monkton, Wootton and numerous other locals and ex-colleagues, curious to know what was going on.

Clarissa Page, the reporter covering the story, held out her recording device, her scruffy little dog regarding us with an intelligent cocking of his head. "What prompted you to call your new business the Wonderland Detective Agency, Ms Liddell?" she asked.

I pulled Hattie close and gave her a hug as the photographer snapped away. "It seemed rather fitting, given that I'll be in an office above the Hat and Dashery. Then there's the coincidence of my name, of course ..."

"It's perfect," Clarissa nodded. "I understand you already had a successful first case?"

"I did. I worked closely with The Ministry of Witches Police Department"—I nodded at Monkton —"and was able to furnish them with evidence that led to the recovery of a murder weapon," I told Clarissa. While Cerys had stayed overnight in hospital, Monkton had searched her desk at work and found the bloody letter opener, wrapped in a scarf in a drawer. Cerys had refused to say a word. She was being held in the hospital wing of Witchwood Scrubbs. Of Makepeace, there had been no sign. "That led to the exoneration of my client."

I beckoned Snitch over, but he widened his eyes in

dread at the idea of having his photo taken and slid into the doorway of the factory opposite. It had been boarded up again. I'd been keeping a careful eye on it over the past few weeks. Where once the rundown structure had appeared benign, now it seemed more menacing.

From the corner of my eye, I spotted the little globe of light that had been plaguing me for weeks, if not months. It hovered, as it always did, just out of reach. Today it was closer than ever before. Ever since Alf had properly drawn my unwilling attention to it, I had begun to allow it to drift nearer.

"Could we take a photo of you unveiling the plaque?" the photographer asked. He had somewhere else to be, so we were all rushing to do his bidding.

"Of course!" I'd had a brass plaque engraved to hang beside the side door, announcing my agency to the world. Hattie had sewn a tiny pair of red velvet curtains to cover it over until the big reveal. I gripped the cord, ready to do the grand unveiling.

"Five! Four!" Monkton started a chant, and Wootton and the rest of the bystanders quickly joined in. "Three! Two! One!"

I tugged and revealed the shining plaque. It wouldn't stay that colour for long. Not in the mucky lanes of Tumble Town. "I now pronounce the Wonderland Detective Agency open for business!" I shouted, beside myself with glee.

There was a roar of approval and a round of applause. I grinned and posed for a couple more photos.

"We're having a few drinks and some nibbles in The Pig and Pepper," Wootton called, and the crowd eagerly began to disperse in that direction. Anything for a vol-au-vent and a sausage on a stick.

"I have a few more questions for you," Clarissa said, "but I'm heading to the reception anyway. I can catch you there, if you like?"

"That's a good idea. I just need to lock up upstairs, and I'll be right with you," I told her.

Hattie, taking that as her cue, caught hold of the pretty young reporter's arm and led her away, a captive audience. "Did you hear about my recent trouble?" I heard her say. "I'm amazed the Hat and Dashery has survived to tell the tale."

I giggled and climbed upstairs to my newly refurbished office. With Snitch's help, Wootton and I had patched holes in the walls and cleaned and painted everywhere. We'd created a proper back office with a little kitchenette where I could hide from the world when I needed to.

In memory of Dodo, I'd kept his desk and chair in situ in the front office, intending to use it myself. You never knew when a secret drawer would come in handy. I'd also purchased another two desks, one for Wootton and one spare. We'd removed most of the bookcases and had thick new carpeting put down in an effort to reduce the noise poor old Hattie had to endure. The walls had been painted a light apricot, and I'd hung white wood slatted blinds at the windows, giving the office a fresher, more contemporary feel. I'd softened the environment further by adding a few more plants—having revived Dodo's, it turned out that Wootton was good with such things—and some colourful art I'd found at Peachstone Market.

I had almost spent up my mother's allowance, but given that I already had six new clients on my list—thanks to Snitch and Monkton spreading the word—the money was beginning to trickle in. Six clients were more than enough. Soon I would be spreading myself too thin. That third desk would come in handy.

But I knew what I had to do.

And now was the time.

I settled myself at Dodo's desk in the front office and concentrated on the small globe of light, so close to me now it was within touching distance.

"Ezra," I called softly. "Welcome."

He didn't need telling twice. He apparated in front of me, beaming from ear to ear. His silver-white hair, weathered face and bulbous nose were as familiar and as dear to me as my own reflection. I noted he was still wearing his old olive trench coat.

"It's about time!" he barked.

"I wasn't ready." Seeing him here in spirit form made his loss so final. It hurt. But now I could accept it.

"But now you are?" he asked.

I nodded.

"You always were a softie, Elise," he said. "You like everyone to perceive you as hardboiled, but in here"— he tapped his chest above his heart—"you're not at all."

I shrugged. "Don't tell anyone."

"So, what have we here?" He began to flit around the office, becoming increasingly excited. "A detective agency, eh? Gone independent, have you?"

"I needed to get away from the Ministry of Witches."

"I can't blame you for that." He collapsed into the seat behind the spare desk. "Need a partner?"

"How did you know?" I winked.

"Izax and Liddell? Liddell and Izax?" He cocked his head to study my reaction.

"A match made in wonderland," I nodded.

WHAT HAPPENS NEXT?

Curious about what happens next?

The Rabbit Hole Murders: Wonderland Detective Agency Book 2

Run rabbit run!

Elise Liddell is no country girl, but she's not averse to the existence of rabbits.

Especially cute and fluffy white ones.

But there's one on the loose in Tumble Town

And that particular sweet bunny turns out to be a harbinger of death …

Every time Elise spots it, she soon discovers another corpse. Keen to help her ex-colleagues at the Ministry of Witches Police Department solve the murders, Elise launches her own investigation alongside the rest of her team at the Wonderland Detective Agency.

The problem is, they're not the only ones trying to get to the bottom of the situation ... and now the hunters have become the hunted.

Available to preorder from Amazon.

HAVE YOU ENJOYED DEAD AS A DODO?

Please leave a review

Have you enjoyed *Dead as a Dodo*?

Please leave me a review on Amazon or Goodreads.

Reviews help spread the word about my work, which is great for me because I find new readers!

And why not join my mailing list to find out more about what I'm up to and what is coming out next? Just pop along to my website and fill in the quick form. You'll find me at jeanniewycherley.co.uk

If you'd like to join my closed author group you'll find it here at www.facebook.com/groups/JeannieWycherleysFiends

Please let me know you've reviewed one of my books
when you apply.

The Complete Wonky Inn Series (in chronological order)

Christmas Cozy Special

Judge, Jury and Jailhouse Rockcakes: Wonky Inn Book 11

A Midsummer Night's Wonky: Wonky Inn Book 12

Spellbound Hound

Ain't Nothing but a Pound Dog: Spellbound Hound Magic and Mystery Book 1

A Curse, a Coven and a Canine: Spellbound Hound Magic and Mystery Book 2

Bark Side of the Moon: Spellbound Hound Magic and Mystery Book 3

Master of Puppies: Spellbound Hound Magic and Mystery Book 4 (TBC)

Wonderland Detective Agency

Dead as a Dodo: Wonderland Detective Agency Book 1

The Rabbit Hole Murders: Wonderland Detective Agency Book 2

Tweedledumb and Tweedledie: Wonderland Detective Agency Book 3 (TBC)

The Municipality of Lost Souls

Midnight Garden: The Extra Ordinary World Novella Series Book 1

Beyond the Veil

Crone

A Concerto for the Dead and Dying

Deadly Encounters: A collection of short stories

Keepers of the Flame: A love story

Non-Fiction

Losing my best Friend

Thoughtful support for those affected by dog bereavement or pet loss

Follow Jeannie Wycherley

Find out more at on the website www.jeanniewycherley.co.uk

You can tweet Jeannie

twitter.com/Thecushionlady

Or visit her on Facebook for her fiction

www.facebook.com/jeanniewycherley

Follow Jeannie on Instagram (for bears and books)

www.instagram.com/jeanniewycherley

Sign up for Jeannie's newsletter on her website

The Creature from the Grim Mire

There's no chance of a quiet life when you've aliens in your attic.

Felicity Westmacott craves solitude.

But something with a hearty appetite is stalking the moor and terrifying the locals.

And things going bump in the night puts paid to her equilibrium.

As does the mysterious appearance of an elderly gentleman.
He claims to be a time traveller.

Obviously as nutty as a fruitcake, he wants her to run a creche.

For baby aliens.

Now her secret's out and other people are interested in Felicity's unusual house guests.

Her 'children' are in terrible danger.

Will Felicity save her young charges? Or will she finish her novel instead?

Find out in *The Creature from the Grim Mire.*

If you've ever wondered what HG Wells got up to in his spare time, you'll love this alien invasion tale set on Dartmoor in South Devon, UK. This is the perfect light-hearted read for lovers of humorous sci-fi mysteries or cozy animal mysteries, or indeed anyone seeking a bit of fun escapism with a cup of tea and a slice of cake.

But keep an eye on your snacks – there are hungry aliens loose. Some of them can eat their body weight in

Custard Creams!

The Creature from the Grim Mire is a collaboration between father and daughter, Peter Alderson Sharp (*The Sword, the Wolf and the Rock*) and Jeannie Wycherley (the Wonky Inn books, *Crone, The Municipality of Lost Souls* etc.).

The Municipality of Lost Souls

Vengeful souls don't stay dead

They taunt the minds of the living until they throw themselves from clifftops.

Yet death turns a profit when you drive ships onto rocks to plunder riches.

Agatha knows one thing for sure: respect the dead.

Especially those who did not die quietly.

Now, a lonely witch has conjured a young sailor's soul. And woken them all.

Only Agatha knows the truth.

She hears it in the whispers drifting across the waves.

She hears it in the crackle of the flames.

And the marauders will stop at nothing to silence her.

Shh ... Listen ...

The Dead Are Coming ...

From the Amazon bestselling author of Crone comes a thoroughly original and spellbinding piece of storytelling. *The Municipality of Lost Souls* is a gothic ghost story set in 1860s England with characters destined to haunt you forever.

For readers of dark fantasy who love witchcraft, magic and a little spookiness. For fans of Daphne du Maurier, Laura Purcell, Michelle Paver and Stacey Halls.

Printed in Great Britain
by Amazon